## Romance in the Spotlight

With all the attention focused on celebrity hookups and breakups these days, we thought it would be exciting to publish a series of novels about love and the pressures of Hollywood fame, which we call ROMANCE IN THE SPOTLIGHT.

In this year's summer series, we asked some of romance's bestselling authors to pen stories of love, intrigue and sizzling romance set against the backdrop of tabloid media and Hollywood.

The final novel in the ROMANCE IN THE SPOTLIGHT series is this month's *Moments Like This* by Donna Hill, a steamy romance about an established actress looking to make the ultimate comeback. Last month's *Love, Lies & Videotape* by Kayla Perrin is a torrid tale of a young actress on the verge of big-time success who is plagued by an unseemly videotape from her past. Sandra Kitt's *Celluloid Memories* is a sultry story about an aspiring screenwriter who finds herself on the brink of success as she tries to unravel a family secret. In June, we kicked off the summer series with *Just the Man She Needs* by Gwynne Forster, which tells the story of two high-profile yet private people, who reluctantly find themselves the subjects of intense publicity.

We hope you enjoy *Moments Like This*. Be sure to buy the other titles in the ROMANCE IN THE SPOTLIGHT series. We welcome your comments and feed                    us an e-mail at www.kimanipr

Enjoy,

Evette Porter
Editor, Arabesque

# DONNA Hill

## Moments Like This

ARABESQUE®

MOMENTS LIKE THIS

An Arabesque novel

ISBN-13: 978-0-373-83019-0
ISBN-10:      0-373-83019-X

www.kimanipress.com

**Printed in U.S.A.**

## Acknowledgment

Thanks go out to all my readers, new and old, who make what I do worthwhile.

# Chapter 1

*Image is everything.* The full-length mirror reflected the gown, the jewels, the hair, the nails, all selected and done with precise deliberation. There was no room for flaws. No one must ever know that beneath the picture-perfect exterior, a war of uncertainty raged within.

"Dominique, hurry up, babe, we're going to be late," Clifton called out from the bottom of the spiral staircase.

"I'm coming, I'm coming. Just one last thing." She stole a final glance. Her reflection smiled at her with practiced confidence.

Clifton adjusted the cuffs of his stark white,

handmade shirt. The diamond links sparkled beneath the light of the overhanging crystal chandelier.

He crossed the black-and-white swirling marble floor to the minibar on the far side of the sunken living room. The off-white walls were adorned with larger-than-life black-and-white photos of Dominique, some from her early days as a supermodel to more recent ones of her in various roles on the big screen.

Clifton poured a glass of brandy and went to stand in front of his favorite photograph—the one of Dominique on the beach at Saint Tropez. She was emerging from the water, her mid-length hair plastered around her face and shoulders. Her hazel eyes were bright and filled with excitement, her body flawless in every way.

She hadn't aged a bit in the years since he'd taken that photo. If anything, her natural beauty had become more alluring.

Clifton took a thoughtful swallow from his glass and tried to think of what excuse he'd offer his lovely wife later on in the evening for leaving her alone.

"Ready."

Clifton turned toward the sound of her voice. Dominique was at the top of stairs. The teal-colored Vera Wang Grecian gown looked fabulous against her cinnamon-colored skin. The deep V-cut gave the observer just enough stimulation without being obvious. He was pleased she'd followed his suggestion and wore the dress he'd chosen for her. He shouldn't be surprised, however, Dominique had always done as he suggested.

"You look incredible," he said sincerely as she gracefully came down the winding stairs, her years of modeling and strutting in front of all-seeing eyes paying off.

A childlike smile moved across her full mouth and woke up the dimple in the right corner of her chin. Diamonds dripped from her ears, caressed her long neck and embraced her left wrist.

"Thank you," she said in that sultry voice her fans had come to know. She walked up to him and kissed him lightly on the lips, enough not to disturb her makeup or leave her lipstick on him.

Clifton finished off his drink and set the empty glass down on the bar.

"Our car is out front."

"I'm so nervous," she confessed as Clifton helped her into the backseat of the limo.

He patted her smooth hand then held it tightly. "You have nothing to be nervous about. No matter what happens this is your night to shine. Just remember what I've always told you, the face you present to the crowd must never reflect your true feelings inside. Give them what they want to see at all times."

She pressed her polished lips together and bobbed her head.

That advice had served her well over the years, she

mused, settling back against the plush leather. The car slowly pulled out of the circular driveway of their Beverly Hills mansion.

She'd come a long way from working as a dental assistant by day and a jazz club waitress by night. The life she lived now was so far removed from her life in Atlanta that often it felt like a dream to her—someone else's life.

There were nights when she'd leap up from sleep, her heart racing and her entire body covered in dampness, believing that she'd lost everything.

Thoughtfully, she reached for Clifton's hand and brought it to her lips. Her husband meant everything to her. As cliché as it sounded, Clifton literally discovered her on the streets of Atlanta. At the time, she'd just turned twenty and wished for some miracle to take the ordinariness out of her days.

"I don't mean to be rude, but have you ever thought of modeling?" he'd asked when he'd stopped her on the street.

"Very original," she replied and started to walk off.

"Wait, here, take this." He handed her a business card.

She barely glanced at it. "Thanks," she muttered, stuck it in the back pocket of her jeans and continued on her way.

"Call me," he shouted.

It was more than a week later when she was gathering her clothes for the laundry that she ran across the card. She stared at the card, contemplating. Clifton Burrell, Fashion Photographer. What harm would it do to call? She did and was surprised to get his assistant on the phone. She made an appointment to come in a week later. Her older sister, Annette, told her she was crazy for going. First, what made her think she was pretty enough to model and second she hoped Dominique didn't wind up on the six o'clock news as another statistic. Dominique went anyway.

She soon learned that Clifton Burrell was very legitimate. He was a photographer for *Elle, Essence* and *Cosmopolitan*, and had connections with several modeling agencies.

"I think you have a lot of potential," he said at that first meeting. "I'd like to take you in to meet the folks over at Ford."

They spent that first afternoon and the following week taking pictures. He wanted the right ones for her portfolio.

Clifton accompanied her to the meeting and within a week she was sent out on her first job.

From there her career blossomed. She did runway and print work, traveled the world to all of the major shows and became friends with some of the biggest names in the business—and Clifton was there every step of the way.

"Would you like some wine, sweetheart?" Clifton asked.

Dominique blinked back the past. Fifteen years

had flown by as swiftly as the landscape outside of the passenger window.

"No." She scrunched up her nose. "I probably shouldn't. Just in case I have to go up on stage."

"One won't hurt. It'll keep you calm."

"Well," she hesitated. "Maybe a little bit."

"That's my girl." He reached for the bottle of white wine in the rack along the side of the car. He poured her a drink and handed her the fragile-stemmed flute. Clifton tapped his glass against hers. "To success."

She smiled.

This was her second Golden Globe nomination. She won her first for her supporting role in *Seven Seas*. But this was her first nomination as a lead actress in a drama and there was already buzz about an Oscar nomination for her performance.

"We were invited to Jamie's after party," Dominique said following a tiny sip of her wine. If she pretended to drink it would at least please Clifton.

He waved his manicured hand in a dismissive fashion. "You know I don't attend those things and neither do you. That's how you wind up in those sleazy tabloids instead of the cover of *Time*."

His tone was so short and condescending that she felt a fool for bringing it up. They never went to any of the parties, rarely socialized except at their home and she did nothing without him. Clifton called it "protecting her image." She considered it snobbish.

He turned to her, softened his voice and his expression. "You're much better than that."

Dominique hid her disappointment behind the beautiful mask she'd perfected and repeated to herself the mantra she'd come to live by: never reveal on the outside what you feel on the inside. *Image is everything.*

The limo pulled up amidst a barrage of flashbulbs and general media frenzy.

The driver hurried around and opened the door.

Clifton stepped out first, waved briefly to the throng of onlookers and photographers, then reached into the car for Dominique's hand. "Ready," he whispered, looking into her eyes. She gave a short nod, set one high-heeled foot out onto to the red carpet and gracefully alighted from the car.

Photographers and fans shouting her name were near deafening from behind the red-velvet ropes.

Dominique tucked her hand into the crook of Clifton's arm and smiled and waved to the crowd.

"Ms. Laws! Ms. Laws!"

She was stopped by an on-camera reporter from *Variety.*

A microphone was shoved at her. "How does it feel to be nominated for best actress?"

"It's incredibly exciting. I'm thrilled to be nominated and to be in the company of such talented actors."

"Ms. Laws, over here!"

"Look over your shoulder, Dominique!"

She turned, waved, smiled and waved some more.

"What's your next project?"

"I have some things that I'm looking at, but nothing has been decided."

"Mr. Burrell, how are you handling your wife's nomination?"

Dominique saw the momentary flash in Clifton's eyes and inwardly cringed.

"My wife deserves all of the accolades she's receiving for her role in *Misdemeanors*. I'm happy with her performance on and off the set." He flashed a broad smile and squeezed Dominique around the waist before planting a kiss on her cheek for the benefit of the camera.

"Well, good luck tonight."

"Thank you so much."

"Oh, and you must tell us who designed that incredible dress."

"Vera Wang."

She felt the almost imperceptible tug on her arm. She waved to the crowd, smiled and continued on into the rotunda of the hall.

"Assholes," Clifton muttered while keeping his face and eyes fully engaged with the crowd. "They all ask the most inane questions."

"They're only doing their jobs."

Just as they entered the rotunda, film director Alan Conners approached them.

"Hello," he greeted, first extending his hand to Clifton.

Clifton covered Alan's hand with both of his and shook it heartily. "Mr. Conners, an honor to meet you. I'm a great fan of your work."

"Thank you." He turned his focus to Dominique and something inside of her shifted out of place. "Ms. Laws, I want to congratulate you on your nomination. You did an incredible job." He took her hand. Lightening struck. They both felt it by the sudden brightness that sparked in their eyes.

"Thank you." Her throat was suddenly dry and she knew that if she were a couple of shades lighter in complexion she would be red in the face.

Alan held her with a look, having released her hand. "Perhaps we'll have an opportunity to work together."

"That would be wonderful. Keep me in mind."

"I certainly will."

"If something does come up, you can always contact me. I handle everything for Dominique," Clifton said, keeping his expression open and inviting.

"I'll do that. Good to meet you." He handed Clifton his card. "And good luck tonight," he said to Dominique. He gave a short nod of his head to both and walked off.

"The nerve of the SOB," Clifton groused.

"What?"

"He was coming on to you—in front of my face!"

"Clif, don't be ridiculous. He was just being nice."

"Being nice, being nice!" He snorted in disgust.

"Does he think that because he made a few films he can come on to another man's wife?"

"He's married."

"You didn't see his wife on his arm did you?"

"Clif, please," she said in an urgent whisper. Her hazel eyes darted around hoping that no one overheard his little tirade. She hated when he got like this and it was happening more and more lately.

"Let's get inside and find our seats," he grumbled.

She let him lead her inside, but it took all of her willpower not to look over her shoulder to catch another glimpse of Alan Conners. Her fingers still tingled from his touch when he held her hand. She smiled and waved as they passed other famous faces in the corridor. Clifton was probably as nervous as she was, she thought, trying to erase the image of Alan's eyes boring into hers. He had just as much at stake. Clifton had single-handedly pulled the strings to get her this part and had worked tirelessly prepping her for the audition. The director didn't want her for the part, but Clifton had convinced him that Dominique could do it—and she had.

Clif took care of her as her husband and as her business manager. He was excellent at both. His minor flare-ups were just inconveniences that she'd become accustomed to.

The doors were open to the great hall where the ceremony was to take place. The place sparkled. The circular tables, covered with white silk tablecloths filled the entire room. The centerpieces were candle votives trimmed in gold. Already food was being served and drinks flowed like the Nile.

They were led to their table in the second row center by a tuxedoed usher.

"At least we get decent seats," he murmured in her ear as he helped her into her chair.

She chuckled. "Clif there's Jack Nicholson and Meryl Streep." She squeezed his hand. Even though she'd been in the movie business for nearly ten years she still got a rush of excitement when she saw actors she'd idolized for most of her life. They were legends in the business and she only hoped she could come somewhere in the vicinity of their stature and longevity.

Halle Berry walked in right in front of Denzel and his wife. *God he was gorgeous.* Their tablemates, the cast from *Misdemeanors*, arrived shortly and Clifton easily slid into his role as the consummate host as if this was his party instead of being an invited guest.

One after another the star-studded lineup of presenters came to the stage to read the lists of nominees and winners. With each passing moment, Dominique's anxiety grew. Finally, the category for Best Performance by an Actress in a Motion Picture— Drama was announced. Once again, they showed clips of the performances.

"And the winner for Best Lead Female Performer in a Drama goes to…"

She held her breath and plastered a smile on her

face, knowing that the cameras were on her and her conominees. The sound of the envelope being ripped opened reverberated like firecrackers in her ears.

"Meryl Streep!"

Dominique beamed with feigned joy and clapped vigorously for Meryl. She even stood and placed a congratulatory kiss on Meryl's cheek as she passed by on her way to accept her Golden Globe. In Dominique's mind, *this* was truly her best performance, acting as if she were thrilled for someone else.

Slowly, Dominique sat down, maintaining her look of composure even as her insides sunk and her head felt light.

The balance of the evening droned on. She was there in body only.

"You should have won," Clifton complained as they were driven back home.

Dominique was actually relieved not to be attending any of the after-parties. She didn't think she could pull off the happy act much longer. That whole *it's great to be nominated* line was totally overrated. Of course all of the interviews following the ceremony focused on her *not* winning and how she felt about it. How do you think I feel? she'd wanted to say, but of course she didn't.

The driver eased the car along the driveway and pulled up in front of the house.

Dominique got out without any help and went

straight inside. Clifton followed shortly after, dismissing the driver for the night.

When he came in, Dominique was at the bar. The celebratory bottle of champagne was still on ice. She was fixing a glass of scotch and soda, something she rarely drank.

"I'm going up to change," he announced.

She turned toward him. "Change?"

"Yes." He checked his watch. "I have a meeting. And I'll be late if I don't hurry."

Her brow wrinkled in confusion. "A meeting? What kind of meeting would you be going to tonight?"

He started for the stairs. "Business."

"But, Clif—"

"I'll be back in a few hours." With that he continued upstairs.

Dominique finished off her drink and fixed another. By the time Clifton came down to leave she had a definite buzz. There were blurry lines around his body.

He gave her a look. "Don't wait up."

Dominique watched him walk out and didn't utter a word. The least he could have done was stay and console her, she thought, sipping her third drink. He knew how much she'd wanted to win and how devastated she was. What was worse, she didn't even have anyone to call, just to talk. Over the years she'd become estranged from her friends and associates. Clifton believed that it was best to keep her camp tight—meaning just him and her. The people she considered friends were her competition, he'd said. When it got down to it, they would think of themselves over her any day. She couldn't call her sister, Annette. They hadn't spoken in ages. So there she sat, alone with nothing to keep her company but a damned good bottle of scotch and her journal.

The next time she saw her husband was the following afternoon. She was so happy just to have another presence in the house, she didn't even care that he'd stayed out all night. At least he was there and she wasn't alone.

# Chapter 2

"You need to take a look at those scripts," Clifton said to her about a week later.

There was a stack of scripts sitting on the desk in her office. They were all crap.

Dominique raised her eyes. "You actually expect me to do any of those?"

Clifton took a step forward. "I expect you to behave like an actress, read scripts and accept roles. It's what you do. Save the wounded diva routine for when you'll really need it."

Heat rose to her head. Her temples pounded. The burn of frustrated tears stung the back of her throat. This was a time when she needed her husband, not her business manager. She needed him to give a damn about how she felt.

"Are you going to let another day go by sitting around in your bathrobe?"

Dominique flung herself up from the couch and marched off to her bedroom. She faced herself in the mirror. Without her expertly coiffed hair and full makeup, Dominique Laws was simply an ordinary woman from Atlanta who'd somehow stumbled into a world bigger and badder than she was. She stared at her reflection and for the first time saw defeat hovering in her eyes, waiting for the opportunity to slide down her cheeks and turn down the corners of her mouth.

The realization startled her. The night of the awards had hit her harder than she would admit to herself. Her ego had been bruised, certainly, but it was her confidence that had become unsteady. Of course it was foolish to put so much stock into one award. There was still the Oscars, the big boys. They'd been talking about her being nominated for months. The names were to be released in a few days.

Dominique drew in a long, deep breath. What was really bothering her? Sure she was disappointed, who wouldn't be? Yet if she was truly honest, at least with herself, she would admit that it went deeper than that.

The real hurt was in the realization of how empty her life and spirit were as a whole and her marriage was in particular. Clifton barely acknowledged the fact that she was hurt and depressed. Instead he acted as if the loss were a personal snub to him. He had left her alone that night, something that still had not been explained.

She picked up a brush from the glass-topped dressing table and ran it through her hair before turning away from the questions her reflection seemed to ask of her.

Dominique went into the study and randomly picked up one of the three scripts that had been sent over for her to consider. Hopefully there was a gem among the pages.

The role the first script envisioned for her was a crack-addicted woman with three kids and no man. In order to support her drug habit, she sends her kids out to steal. She put that one aside and picked up another one. The next one was a stripper. She didn't read past the first five pages. In the next one the role was a teenager whose dream was to appear in a music video to escape a life in the projects. She couldn't pull off being a teenager with all the makeup in the world.

Disgusted, she dropped the script unceremoniously on the floor. The thud sounded like a slamming door.

She leaned her head back against the cushion of the chair and stared up at the stucco ceiling. *They have got to be kidding.* Those scripts underscored every stereotype of black women and black life: the poor, the uneducated, the trifling. There had to be something out there for her, something that matched the talent she knew she had.

Dominique briefly shut her eyes; without warning, an image of Alan Conners emerged. The suddenness startled her. Not so much seeing him in her mind's eye the way he was the night of the awards, but how conjuring up the image of him made her feel. It was disconcerting.

In her thirty-five years she'd only been with four men—more boys than men—before Clifton. She'd been captivated by Clifton's maturity, charm and his devotion to her. He was the first man to make her understand the true power and passion of sex and what a man could do to and for a woman's body. And from the moment they moved from business associates to friends to lovers to husband and wife, she'd never looked at another man—nor fantasized about one. That made her sudden fascination with Alan Conners all the more disturbing. Since the night she'd met him in the rotunda at the Golden Globes, he would leap into her mind at any given moment.

"New technique in reading a script?"

Dominique's eyes flashed open and she felt flush all over as if she'd been caught doing something wrong. She ran her tongue across her lips. "I was thinking about the scripts." She got up from the chair and came to stand in front of him. She held his wrists loosely. "They're awful, Clif, and I'm being kind. One of them wants me to play a teenager for a music video. Come on."

Clifton shifted his body. Dominique released his wrists.

"You're an actress, Dominique. A black actress. Roles worthy of your talent are few and far between. We both know that."

"So I should settle for whatever piece-of-shit script they send to me?"

"*You* make the role yours. *You* make them believe. Most people hate their jobs. Why should you be any different?"

"Is that some kind of consolation?"

"Listen, if you hate them that much, don't do them. Simple. We'll wait for something else. Besides, once you get nominated for that Oscar, they'll be beating down our door."

That brought a smile that put a light in her eyes. *The Oscars.* "You're right, of course," she said and walked up behind him. She slid her arms around his waist and pressed her head against his back. "I'm going to wait for the right project. There's no need to jump on something. We certainly aren't hurting for money and taking the wrong role could do me more harm than good. You've said as much to me yourself."

Clifton extricated himself from her hold. "Then I better get busy and find you the right project." He turned to her and kissed her lightly on the tip of her nose then walked out.

For the briefest moment, Dominique felt a chill of uncertainty that went straight to her center. She glanced at the empty doorway then shook her head in dismissal. She was being silly and overly sensitive about nothing.

Gathering herself together, she headed for the kitchen. Marcia, the cook and general housekeeper, was busy preparing the menu for dinner.

"Good morning, Mrs. Burrell."

"Hi, Marcia. I wanted to give you the day off."

"Off?" She frowned in concern.

"With pay, of course. I wanted to fix dinner for Mr. Burrell tonight, spend some time together."

"Are you sure? I mean I can fix whatever you want. I—"

"No, no, it's fine. Really," she said with a reassuring smile. "Go on home to your family and I'll see you tomorrow."

Marcia untied her apron. "Thank you, Mrs. Burrell. My house will be glad to see me."

Dominique smiled. "I'm sure."

Marcia neatly folded her apron and put it in the drawer where she kept it next to the sink. "I'll see you tomorrow. Have a nice evening."

"Thanks."

Once Dominique heard the front door close she looked around at what Marcia had begun to prepare and picked up where she'd left off. She adjusted the wall panel dial near the refrigerator and soft music filtered into the kitchen from hidden speakers.

Dominique hummed along. This is what she and

Clifton needed, she thought as she seasoned the wild salmon steaks, a night alone, just the two of them.

Clifton called about eight that evening to inform her that he wouldn't be home for dinner. He had a business meeting in the valley and that she shouldn't wait up.

Dominique ate alone in the massive dining room, lighted candles and a floral centerpiece her company.

The morning that the Oscar nominations were to be announced, Dominique was up before dawn. She puttered around in the kitchen fixing a pot of coffee. Any minute the phone would ring and she would be informed that she'd been nominated in the best actress category.

Her heart pounded and pounded waiting for the call. Finally she crept back into the bedroom, trying not to wake Clifton, and turned on the television news. The local announcer said that the Oscar nominations were just being announced and they'd air it live from the Shrine Auditorium right after the commercial break.

"Clif, Clif." She gently shook his shoulder.

He muttered and mumbled before rubbing his eyes and opening them. "What's the matter?"

"They're getting ready to announce the nominations," she said, trying to temper the excitement in her voice.

He struggled to sit up in bed. He pulled her next to him. "This is your big moment."

She squeezed his hand just as the screen flashed to a podium at the Shrine. Rob Lowe and Kyra Sedgwick were making the presentations.

Dominique could barely breathe as she listened to one category after the next being announced.

"The nominations for Best Actress in a Leading Role are…"

# Chapter 3

Dominique sat in dazed silence. The moment was surreal. All this time, all the work, all the hope. Gone in an instant. She couldn't move.

Clifton got up from the bed, went to the television and shut it off before storming into the bathroom. The door slammed with such force that the beveled mirror that hung over the dresser rattled against the wall. Dominique's body jerked in response.

She looked around the room as if seeing it for the first time. Slowly she got up. Five names, five contenders, none of them were her. At first she thought she'd simply missed hearing her name being called. But she hadn't. She drew in a shaky breath.

The phone rang. Mindlessly she picked it up. "Hello?"

"Ms. Laws, this is Janice Rogers from *Variety*. The nominations for the Oscars were just announced. What are your feelings about not getting a nomination?"

Her stomach roiled. She inhaled through her nose.

"I am thrilled for all of the wonderful actors who were nominated. And I wish them the best of luck."

"Why do you think you were overlooked?"

She shut her eyes. "The Academy can't pick everyone," she said, struggling to keep her composure.

"*Misdemeanors* was nominated for Best Picture. Why do you think they avoided recognizing your role in making the picture as good as it was?"

"I really can't get into the heads of the Academy. Thanks for calling." She hung up.

Clifton came out of the bathroom still rubbing his face with a washcloth. "Who was that?"

"A reporter from *Variety*."

The phone rang again. She flinched. Clifton brushed by her and snatched up the phone.

He listened for a moment. "We think it's wonderful." He slammed down the phone.

"Another reporter?"

"*Entertainment Weekly*."

Again the phone rang.

"God!" She arched her head back. "This is going to go on all day."

Clifton disconnected the phone. "I'll prepare a

statement for the press and leave it at that." He
stalked back into the bathroom and shut the door.

"They're obviously deaf, dumb and blind," Clifton
complained as he stormed back and forth across the
tiled floors of the kitchen, still seething more than an
hour later. "How in the hell can you nominate the
picture, the director, best actor and supporting actor
and actress and not nominate the female lead?"

Hearing the words out loud only drove the knife
deeper. It was like a slap in the face. "Here, take
that." All morning she'd relived that moment and the
shock was still as fresh now as it was hours ago. She
couldn't imagine how many calls must have come
through since they'd shut off the phone.

"The hell with it." He dumped his cold coffee in the
sink and tossed the cup in behind it. It cracked into
razor-sharp shards against the stainless steel sink,
which only fueled his anger. "I'm going to see Manny.
He needs to get on the job and find you some work."

Manny Breevort was her agent. They'd worked
together for years. As agents go, he was one of the
best and had been very successful in finding her some
of the best roles available. She'd had a string of criti-
cally acclaimed successes as a result of his tena-
ciousness and ability to find hidden gems. But lately,
if the scripts she was getting were any indication,
Manny was definitely slipping.

Clifton left the house with a thud. Marcia was

at the market and Dominique knew she couldn't spend another minute rambling around alone in that big house.

She dressed as inconspicuously as possible, in a baby-blue jogging outfit, white sneakers and a baseball cap. Instead of taking the Mercedes with her vanity plates, she opted for the black Mustang and drove just outside of town to her favorite outdoor restaurant. She'd found it quite by accident several years earlier and was thrilled to discover that no celebrities or autograph hounds frequented the place. It was small, inconspicuous and off the beaten path. Just the kind of place she needed right about now. The last thing she wanted was to be recognized and quizzed ad nauseam about the Oscar nominations. She shuddered to think what would ultimately end up in the papers and every entertainment show on the planet.

She parked her car along the winding curb and got out. The day was yet another exquisite, California-sunshine day. Smog was nearly imperceptible and for miles greenery and rolling hills could be seen. Young tan bodies strutted their stuff, getting warmer and browner beneath the blazing sunshine.

Dominique crossed the street and walked toward the café. She stood outside for a moment studying the sandwich board of daily specials.

A young waitress came up to her. "Would you like a table inside or out?"

She looked no older than seventeen, Dominique

observed, full of youthful expectancy. "Outside would be great. Thanks."

"Let me show you to a table." She led Dominique to a table at the far end of the café, beneath an umbrella. She handed Dominique a menu. "Can I get you something to drink?"

"Sparkling water with lemon, please."

"Ice?"

"Yes, please. Thank you."

"Coming right up."

Dominique watched her walk away with the little bounce in her step and remembered when she was young and full of optimism. Sometimes she felt like all she had to do was open a door, step to the other side and, like *Alice in Wonderland,* walk into a new world— or at the very least, her old life—where things were simple. If only it were that uncomplicated and magical.

The waitress returned with her water and set it down on the table. "Ready to order?"

"Yes." She scanned the list one last time before putting it down and looking up to tell the waitress— whose name tag read Tammy—what she wanted.

"It'll be about fifteen minutes."

Dominique nodded. Another thing she appreciated about this place was that the employees were discrete or perhaps too young to know who she was. For all the times she'd eaten there, she'd never been approached for an autograph, even though she was often greeted by name.

She slipped out of her hoodie and hung it on the back of the chair. Immediately, she felt the beat of the sun on her back and arms. She reached into her purse and took out a book. Reading was her guilty pleasure. What she regretted was that she had so little time to read for enjoyment. It was either a script, a contract, some sort of business deal, reviews or e-mails that she usually read.

Reading a good book, to her, was the equivalent of taking a trip without a ticket. A really great novel could make you forget your own troubles and enter into the world of someone else.

She opened to the page where she'd left off. Dominique sipped her water as she read, absorbed the healing rays of the sun, relaxed in the soothing atmosphere. Slowly, the knot that had formed in her stomach began to loosen and the pounding in her head dulled to a minor throb.

She almost felt like her old self again as she gradually became immersed in the novel and the plight of Alex Cross, one of her favorite characters.

The waitress returned with her food and when she glanced up, she noticed a couple getting out of a car across the street. It was Alan Conners and a woman. She watched them from beneath the brim of her cap until they disappeared around the corner, Alan's hand at the small of her back.

Dominique wasn't sure if she'd exhaled so deeply from relief or disappointment. Relief that he hadn't noticed her and approached, or disappointment that he was with someone. She stared at her grilled chicken salad and pushed the food around the plate with her fork. Why should she care one way or the other if he was with someone? She knew he was married and the woman could have been his wife, whom she'd never met, or a client.

She speared a piece of chicken and put it in her mouth, chewing thoughtfully. What did it matter? She wasn't mentally up to holding a conversation anyway.

Reading and eating, she whiled away about an hour. By this time the café was beginning to get crowded and although the waitress didn't come right out and ask her to leave, she had dropped by her table more than once to ask if there was anything else she needed. She'd been given her check quite some time ago.

Knowing that she'd worn out her welcome, she signaled for Tammy who gladly took her bill and her credit card.

Dominique gathered up her things, trying to decide what she wanted to do next. It would be so great to have a girlfriend to hang out with, window shop or swap running commentaries on the people on the street. She smiled sadly as she got behind the wheel of her car.

She'd become so isolated over the years, allowing her entire existence to revolve around her career and Clifton. Never before had her solitude hit her as hard

as it had during the past few weeks. She pulled out
and came to a stop on the next street at the red light.
While she waited for the light to change, Alan
Conners crossed right in front of her. The suddenness
of his appearance caused her to push down even
harder on the brake, making the car lurch forward
before settling down. Alan didn't seem to notice and
continued across the street.

Horns honked behind her. She glanced up. The
light was green. Shaking her head. she quickly
released the brake and zipped across the intersection.

Damn, what were the odds of that happening,
not once but twice? The second time, however, he
was alone. Maybe it was a client, she thought,
driving aimlessly around Los Angeles. Why did
she feel good about that assumption? *You know the
answer,* her conscience taunted; if it was a client,
then the two of them being together was nothing
more than business.

For the rest of the afternoon, she kept looking
over her shoulder as she strolled along Rodeo Drive,
she checked the reflections in store windows,
thinking that at any moment Alan was going to ma-
terialize once again.

Stopping in a small high-end boutique with a French
name she didn't dare try to pronounce, Dominique
made a few purchases. She certainly didn't need them,
but it gave her something to do. When she stepped
outside, her small shopping bag in hand, the once sunny

day had turned gray and ugly. Thick clouds hovered above, waiting to open up and douse those below.

She hurried back to her car just as the first drops of rain began to fall. Driving in the rain along the winding narrow roads to her house in the hills always unnerved her. Clifton said she was silly and that she'd been driving long enough not to be frightened by a little rain. That didn't stop her from gripping the steering wheel as the rain fell, building to a steady deluge.

By the time she reached home, her fingers were stiff and her knees wobbly. She darted into the house, but couldn't avoid getting drenched even in the few steps to the front door.

She shook off the water as she went inside and was quickly greeted by the aroma of food cooking and Marcia.

"Marcia, what are you doing here? Today is your day off," she said, removing the wet cap from her head. She ran her fingers through her hair.

"Oh, Mr. Burrell called me at home. He asked me to come and prepare dinner. He's expecting guests tonight."

"Guests?" She jerked her head back and frowned. "He didn't tell me about any guests."

Marcia shrugged. "That's what he said, ma'am."

"Did he say what time these guests were expected?"

"Eight o'clock, ma'am."

Dominique checked her watch. It was almost six.

She blew out a sigh. "Thanks, Marcia. I better get myself together." She headed upstairs to her bedroom.

Dumping her shopping bag on the ottoman, she started to strip out of her damp clothing and went to run a bath. At least she wouldn't spend the rest of the evening alone, she thought as she added bath salts to the water.

While she soaked in the tub she tried to picture what she had in her closet that would be appropriate for an impromptu dinner. It would help tremendously if she knew who was coming.

Dominique quickly finished with her bath and was stepping out of the steamy room when Clifton walked in.

"Aren't you ready yet? Our guests will be here shortly."

She took the towel from around her hair and let her hair fall down around her shoulders. She threw him an angry glare. "It would have been nice if I was the first to know that we were having guests for dinner, Clif. I only walked in a few minutes ago."

The sound of his footfalls were submerged in the thick milk-chocolate colored carpet. He crossed the room to his dresser, snatched off his tie and tossed it on top. He began unbuttoning his shirt.

"Then I suggest you hurry up. You know it takes you forever to get ready." Finally he turned to face her. "Where were you all day?"

"Just out. I didn't want to spend the day alone."

When he made no comment, she continued. "Do you mind telling me who's coming or is it a surprise?"

"Manny and his wife Evelyn. He managed to finagle a meeting with Alan Conners, so he's coming and bringing his wife—thank God." He unbuckled his belt, snapped it out of the loops and hung it on the rack in his cedar closet. "At least I won't have to worry about him ogling you through dinner." He stepped out of his shoes and put them in a fleece shoe bag. "I'm going to take a quick shower." He walked past her and into the bathroom, shutting the door behind him.

Dominique concentrated on breathing slowly in the hope that her racing heartbeat would return to normal. Alan Conners was coming here? She walked over to the bed and sat down on the edge. Three times in one day. Hopefully the three-strikes rule wouldn't apply and she wouldn't make a simpleton of herself during dinner.

Did his coming here mean that he had a role for her to consider? She bit down on her bottom lip. If so, that would make the fiasco of the past few weeks become a quick and distant memory.

She hopped up from the bed, hurried across the room and flung open her closet. The array of clothing was suddenly daunting. She walked in and ran her hand along the racks of clothing. She didn't want to be too dressy and certainly not too casual. Finally she settled on an eggshell-white silk sweater with a V-cut in back and a pair of matching silk pants.

She was putting on a black thong when Clifton stepped out of the bathroom. She turned in his direction. He gave her half-naked body a brief glance and proceeded to get dressed.

Dominique lifted her chin ever so slightly and turned away to finish dressing.

When had it gotten to this? she thought as she put on a light coating of lip gloss. When had their relationship deteriorated so that his eyes didn't even sparkle when he saw her bare breasts? Granted, she wasn't porn-star material, but her breasts were firm and upright and more than a handful. She worked hard at keeping her body in shape, not only for her career but for her husband. She tried to remember the last time they'd made love—not had sex, but made love—and she couldn't. Which was probably why she was so taken—well, turned on by—Alan. She was starved for physical attention.

Dominique made the last touches to her hair, which she decided to wear in a loose knot at the nape of her neck. Now that she'd arrived at the only logical conclusion for her attraction to Alan Connors, she could put it out of her mind and get through dinner as the lady of the house, not some sex-starved housewife on the make.

Taking one last look at herself in the mirror, she headed downstairs to check on dinner and await her guests.

# Chapter 4

Marcia had set a wonderful table in the formal dining room and had prepared seafood as well as a meat dish for the main course. Salad plates were already on the table with a bottle of wine chilling along with their best crystal and china.

Dominique moved the vase of fresh flowers from the sideboard and placed it on the dining table. She took another quick look around. Everything was perfect. She left the dining room to go into the front of the house where they would have hors d'oeuvres prior to the main course.

Marcia had set out smoked salmon, imported crackers and caviar. Dominique hated caviar, but

Clifton insisted it was a *must-have* at any dinner party, no matter how small.

She drew back the drapes that covered one side of the room to reveal a magnificent view of the mountains. Shortly, Clifton came downstairs, adjusting his open-front shirt as he did.

When she looked at him, in control, handsome and so virile, she remembered all the reasons why she'd fallen so hard for him. She wanted the man she'd married. The man who couldn't keep his hands or his eyes off her.

She met him at the foot of the staircase. She raised up slightly and kissed him tenderly on the mouth. "I love you, you know," she whispered.

He looked into her eyes. "Love you, too. You look great."

The tiny compliment warmed her deeply. "Thank you." She took his hand and they walked into the living room together.

"Clif, I was thinking that maybe we could make some time to go away together, get things back on track with us."

He let go of her hand and continued toward the bar. He fixed himself a scotch. "I didn't realize we were off track." He returned the bottle then took a quick swallow. He briefly closed his eyes savoring the drink as it warmed its way down his throat.

"You have to admit things have been…different between us."

He didn't comment.

"Don't you think so?"

"No. Not really. We've both been very busy. We have your career to think about."

She came up to him, cupped his chin and forced him to look at her. Her eyes roamed across his face. "We have our marriage to think about, too."

"We'll see," he said in a dismissive tone before moving away from her grasp.

Dominique's shoulders sagged as he walked away. She turned to the bar. Maybe she needed a drink, too. At least that would warm her insides.

Moments later the bell rang and the first of their dinner guests arrived. It was Manny and his wife Evelyn. Dominique realized her hands were shaking slightly as she embraced Evelyn.

"You look marvelous," Evelyn said, holding Dominique at arm's length to observe her. "What the hell does the Academy know," she scoffed and kissed Dominique's cheek.

Evelyn Breevort was a statuesque, five-foot-ten-inch beauty; blond, blue-eyed and buxom. The three Bs that denote success. A former Miss Texas U.S.A., she still carried herself as if she were competing for the next pageant. Dominique wasn't sure what Evelyn did for a living other than spend Manny's money, but she always seemed to be involved in some "cause" or the other, which she was filling Dominique's ear with now.

"You must become a part of this," she was saying. "It's simply dreadful…"

Dominique had one ear on Evelyn and one eye on the door.

"We're holding a banquet in three months to raise money. It would be great if you were on the decorating committee."

Dominique blinked and focused on Evelyn. "Committee?"

"Yes, we could use all the help we can get. That is of course if you aren't working on your next film."

Evelyn had the uncanny ability to make you feel guilt-ridden without even batting her long fake lashes.

"I'll have to let you know, Evelyn. It sounds wonderful." Whatever it was.

"So what are you working on these days?" She lowered her voice to a pseudo whisper as if they were real girlfriends. "Is it a secret?"

"I have a few things I'm considering."

Her pencil-thin brows rose. "Really?"

"You sound surprised."

"No." She waved her hand. "It's just that I thought you might want to take some time off after…well, you know."

"The best way to keep your skills up is to get back on the horse once you've been thrown off." She forced a smile.

"True. I hope it's something worth your talent."

She thought of the dismal scripts she had on her desk. "I believe so."

The doorbell chimed and Dominique's heart slammed in her chest.

Marcia went to the door. Dominique held her breath.

Alan walked in accompanied by his wife. Clifton left the side of Manny and went to greet them. He shook Alan's hand vigorously.

"Thanks for coming. Welcome."

"This is my wife, Adrienne."

"Pleasure to meet you. Come in and make yourselves at home." He ushered them into the main room and Manny followed.

She definitely was not the woman Dominique saw him with earlier. Adrienne Conners could easily be a body double for Naomi Campbell. She had the same look, the same haughty attitude and demeanor. Her smile never quite reached her doe-shaped eyes, however. And if it was a weave she was wearing, it was a damned good one. The silky ink-black hair hung straight as an arrow down to the center of her back.

"Good to see you again," Dominique said to Alan, shaking his hand. He introduced his wife. Dominique turned to Adrienne. "It's good to meet you. Please make yourselves comfortable. Dinner will be served shortly."

"Beautiful home you have," Alan commented.

"Thank you."

"Who's your interior designer?" Adrienne asked with a slight Southern drawl.

"Actually, I did it myself."

She looked mortified. "Yourself? But why?"

Dominique was momentarily thrown off guard by the question. "Well…I like doing it. I thought no one else would know what I wanted better than I did."

Adrienne flicked a brow. "I see." She flounced off toward the bar.

Alan smiled sheepishly. "I think it's great," he said for only her ears.

"Al, do you want a drink?" Adrienne called out.

"Let me do that for you," Clifton said, rushing over.

"Nothing for me, right now."

Alan and Dominique were left to face each other.

"I was sorry to hear that you didn't get the nod. You really deserved it," he said.

"Thank you. I appreciate that. Especially coming from you. I'm a great admirer of your work."

"I try." He grinned and she noticed how his eyes crinkled at the corners. "How long have you lived here?"

"About eight years. Are you in the area?"

"Only sometimes. We have a house here, but I'm only on the West Coast when I'm shooting a film or for some event."

"Oh, so where do you live?"

"In Atlanta and New York, mostly."

"Really, I grew up in Atlanta."

"No kidding," his expression grew animated. "A

homegirl." He chuckled and it drew Adrienne's attention. She sauntered over, drink in hand.

"What's so funny?"

"Dominique was telling me she grew up in the ATL."

"Are you from Atlanta, Adrienne?"

"No. Savannah."

"Beautiful city."

"Hmm." She took Alan's arm. "Will you excuse us for a minute," she said to Dominique, even as she hustled her husband away.

"Sure," she murmured to their retreating backs.

"She's a piece of work," Evelyn said coming up behind her.

Dominique turned around. "Why do you say that?"

"She's snide and condescending. You should hear how she was talking about the artwork on the walls. You would think she'd have a little more courtesy in someone else's home." She rolled her eyes.

Dominique turned her gaze in the direction of Alan and his wife, they appeared to be in a heated exchange although they kept their voices to thunderous whispers.

"Wonder what that's all about," Evelyn said, watching them.

Marcia walked into the main room and came up to Dominique. "Dinner is ready, ma'am."

Dominique clasped her shoulder. "Thank you—" she lowered her voice "—especially for putting this together at the last minute."

Marcia smiled. "It's fine." She turned and walked out.

"Dinner is ready," Dominique announced.

"In the dining room," Clifton said, leading the way with Manny at his side.

Everyone followed and Marcia began bringing out the trays of food: grilled wild salmon steaks sprinkled with lemon and parsley, roasted chicken, French-cut green beans in Marcia's special cream sauce, sautéed yellow rice with pearl onions and baked potatoes with chives.

"The salad dressings are on the serving table in the glass cruets," Dominique said. "Please help yourselves."

The guests did as instructed then made their way to the table.

"Sit anywhere," Dominique said.

Once everyone fixed their salads, they took their places at the table and Dominique tingled all over as Alan slid into the chair next to her. As always, Clifton sat at the head of the table.

Conversation flowed easily, from politics to religion to the latest gossip, ultimately ending in the entertainment field.

"Dominique is ready to do something big to follow up *Misdemeanors*," Clifton was saying.

Dominique wanted to shrink into her designer shoes. Being the center of attention in a film or on a stage was one thing, but up close and this personal always made her incredibly uncomfortable. Clifton worked hard to sculpt her into a diva, but at her core she was a simple woman with simple needs and wants.

For her, acting had been a way to come out of her shell, become one of those people she imagined in her mind. Modeling was the same thing—all pretend and illusion. And when she stepped off the screen or the runway, she just wanted to be Nikki, not Dominique Laws, supermodel cum actress. Of course, Clifton wouldn't hear of it and tooted her horn for her every chance he got, whether his audience wanted to hear it or not.

Dominique's face burned with embarrassment as Clifton went on about her talent and what fools the Academy and the Golden Globe judges were not to have recognized it.

Everyone chimed in to second Clifton's assessment.

Maybe there would be a freak earthquake, Dominique thought, that would bring this moment to an abrupt end.

Mercifully, dinner drew to a close and all the guests returned to the living room. Since it was such a nice night, Clifton suggested they take their after-dinner drinks out to the patio by the pool.

"This is an incredible view," Alan said, walking up next to Dominique.

"Yes, it is," she said, drawing in a long breath and gazing out at the mountains in the distance. She turned to him. "I'm really sorry about Clifton going on and on like that."

Alan grinned. "You should be thrilled that your husband is behind you that way. Many men get intimidated by wives who either have power or are in the spotlight. Yours obviously isn't." He sipped his drink.

"How long do you plan to stay in L.A.?"

"Actually I'm leaving in the morning to go to New York for a few weeks."

"Oh." She hid her disappointment behind the rim of her glass.

"Alan."

He turned at the sound of his wife's voice. She was walking toward them.

"I'm ready to leave."

He put his drink down on the table then turned to Dominique. He smiled warmly. "It was good to see you again. Thank you for inviting us."

"You're more than welcome. It was our pleasure." She extended her hand to Adrienne, who shook it loosely. "Nice to meet you."

Adrienne barely smiled. She clasped Alan's upper arm and they walked away.

Dominique watched them as they said their good nights. Clifton walked them to the door. When he returned he came up to Dominique.

"Well, did you at least try to find out what movies he's working on that you would be right for?"

"We didn't talk about movies. We didn't really talk about anything."

"Well, you damn sure were talking about something over here." He stared at her waiting for a response.

"I barely had time to say much of anything, Clif. His wife came over and said she wanted to leave. All I had a chance to ask was how long he planned to be in L.A."

Clifton's jaw clenched in annoyance. "Do I have to do everything?" He threw her one hard look, turned and walked away.

Dominique lowered her head. What had been a somewhat pleasant evening took a sudden downturn. All she wanted to do was go to bed.

"We're going to get ready to go," Evelyn said, interrupting Dominique's thoughts.

Dominique blinked and focused on Evelyn. She smiled. "Thanks so much for coming. I hope you enjoyed yourselves."

"Of course. Can't beat a free dinner," she joked. "Are you okay? You seem a little tense or something."

"No, I'm fine. A bit tired, but fine."

She patted her hand. "Get some rest and think about joining the committee. We'd love to have you."

"I will. Promise." She kissed Evelyn's cheek. "I'll call you."

Evelyn wagged a finger at her. "Be sure you do." She went to join her husband.

Dominique entered the house and went into the

dining room with the intention of cleaning up, but Marcia had already taken care of it and everything was back in perfect order.

"I'm going out for a while," Clifton announced.

Dominique turned to face him. "Tonight? Where are you going?"

"Out. I have some business to take care of."

"At this hour? Clif—"

"I really don't have time for this, Dominique. I'll see you when I get back." With that he walked out before she could protest further.

"Fine," she said to the empty room. "Go." She went to the bar in the next room and fixed a drink. Maybe it would help her to sleep.

She took her drink up to her bedroom, undressed and curled up in bed after retrieving her journal from the top shelf of her closet. Alone again. She opened to a blank page and started to write while she sipped her drink. The first drink didn't help, all it did was make her think about how lonely she was. She poured her feelings onto the page and more alcohol down her throat. The second drink wasn't much better. It had her wishing that she were free and that Alan Conners was as well.

# Chapter 5

"Aren't you going to talk to me?" Adrienne complained as they drove home.

"About what?" Alan kept his eyes on the road. He felt one of her tantrums coming and he wasn't in the mood.

"Anything. Like maybe why you were ogling that woman."

He snapped his head in her direction for a moment. "What woman?"

"The one with the big boobs and blue eyes," she said, her tone taking on a nasty edge.

Alan chortled. "You're kidding, right?"

"I saw the way you were looking at her." Her

voice began to rise in pitch. "The way you always do when we go out."

"Don't start, Adrienne. I mean it."

"Mean it," she huffed. Her eyes widened. She flung her hair across her shoulder. "It's always the same thing with you, Alan. And when you thought I wasn't paying attention you were all up in the queen bee's face."

"Enough!"

"Why do you treat me like this? I'm your wife!" She began to cry.

Alan wished that he could close his eyes and when he opened them his eight-year marriage to Adrienne would be a bad dream. But he knew that would never happen.

He'd loved her once, at least he thought he had. But days like this one made him feel it could have never been possible.

In the beginning, Adrienne was sweet, loving, sexy. He fell hard for her. She was the younger sister of his best friend and business partner, Brian. But two years into their marriage her sweet ways became cloying, her loving attitude turned obsessive, and the sexy woman who would do anything to please him in bed morphed into a woman who used sex as a weapon.

Her moods swings and obsessive, clinging, paranoid behavior had gotten worse in the past year and a half, but she refused to get help. Instead, she seemed to prefer to make his life a living hell, blaming him for her ups and downs.

He was tired, so very tired.

"I can't wait to get away from here," she continued to complain. She folded her arms tightly across her chest. "I want to go back home to Georgia."

Alan didn't bother to respond. He knew if he did, no matter what he said, it would turn into something else. No one knew what was going on in his marriage, not even Brian. So many times he'd wanted to tell Brian, but Brian adored his sister and Alan knew he'd never believe him. He'd even considered getting a divorce, but Brian controlled the purse strings to their production company. If he pulled out of his marriage, he might as well kiss his company goodbye.

Maybe things would be better in Atlanta. Adrienne generally seemed to calm down when she was in familiar settings. She had her friends and family there and would at least give him space to breathe.

"Dominique said she was from Atlanta," Adrienne said suddenly. "Did you know her from back home?"

"No. We never met before."

"Are you sure?"

"Yes, Adrienne, I'm sure."

She pouted. "I saw her watching you," she said. "I know she wants to take you from me. I just know it." That statement set off a new rush of irrational tears.

"Adrienne, she wasn't watching me." But he'd been watching her, every move she made. He'd hung on her every word, imagined her silky body moving beneath the soft fabric of her clothing. Even now he could still hear her voice, her laughter. That tight feeling in his groin kicked up again, just like it had the first time he'd seen Dominique. It was only the two drinks he'd had that kept it under control tonight. There was something in her eyes that opened up the door to her soul and he saw something there, the same thing he saw when he looked in the mirror— unhappiness. "She was being a good hostess, that's all," he added. His penis jerked and he shifted slightly in his seat.

Adrienne snatched a look in his direction. "I know it's more than that," she said, her tone turning ominous and dark. "I can tell. So don't lie to me. I hate it when you lie to me!"

He pulled up to the driveway of their home and brought the car around to the front of the house. He gripped the steering wheel. "Adrienne, I can't do this. I won't." He adjusted himself in the seat to look at her. Her mascara had run, leaving a black trail down her cheeks. His heart twisted for a moment. He reached out to caress her cheek with the tip of his finger. "Baby, please. You've got to get some help. We can't go on like this. It's killing our marriage."

Adrienne leaned around the gears and wrapped her arms around his neck. "Don't leave me, Alan, please. I can't live without you. I love you so much. You're my life. Oh, God, don't leave me."

He closed his eyes and held her. Her soft scent wafted around him and his heart softened. Where was the woman he married?

"Come on, sweetheart, let me put you to bed." He got out and helped her out of the car.

She leaned her weight against his body. Alan scooped her up and carried her inside. Her head was buried in his neck and he knew by the time he got her upstairs she would be asleep. These episodes seemed to drain all the energy out of her. Then she would wake up and be perfectly fine— until the next time.

At least for tonight he could rest.

The following morning, Alan was up early and in his home office. Adrienne was still asleep. He was going over the details of some financing for a project that he and Brian wanted to work on when the phone rang.

"Conners."

"Hey man, it's Brian."

Alan leaned back in his seat and grinned. "Hey yourself. Whats up?"

"Just checking in. You have a chance to go over the financing yet?"

"Actually that's what I'm doing now. On first pass, it looks pretty good. But I want to check out the fine print."

Brian had been responsible for much of Alan's

success as a director. It was Brian who had sought out the financing for projects that ultimately led to Alan becoming the director. Over the past six months, they'd been working hard on getting enough capital to launch their own production company. The bare bones of it was set up, but they needed money and plenty of it.

"When are you heading back?"

"We have a flight scheduled for tomorrow morning. We'll be landing around noon."

"Great. I'll meet you at the airport. And how is my beautiful sister?"

Alan's spirits took a nosedive. "Good. She's fine. Still getting her beauty rest, but I'll tell her that you called."

"I was thinking about grilling up some steaks tomorrow night on the deck. You guys come on over for dinner."

"Sure. I'll let A know."

"Okay, buddy. See you tomorrow. Any change in your flight, just give me a holla."

"Will do."

He hung up the phone. Yeah, maybe being back in the comfort of her family would help Adrienne. Brian always had a way of bringing out the best in his sister. It would simply kill him to know what was really going on. But if it continued, Alan would have no choice but to tell him. And the most recent episodes weren't even the worst of them.

* * *

Dominique sat outside Manny's office waiting for him to finish his phone call. She chatted idly with his assistant, Doris. Her mind, however, was on the call she'd received from Manny that morning, asking her to make time to come in and see him. He refused to discuss it over the phone, said it would be best in person.

She didn't like the sound of it.

Doris's intercom buzzed. "You can go on in," she said.

"Thanks. Talk to you later." Dominique got up and walked into Manny's office.

He was seated behind his massive desk. All along his wall were photographs of him with his famous clients in a variety of settings from yacht parties to red carpet events to private dinners.

Manny was the definition of a Hollywood agent—from the slick, handsome looks and polished dress to his fast-talking, salesman-like spiels.

He stood. "Come in, Dom. Have a seat." He came from behind his desk, kissed her lightly on the cheek and held a chair for her.

Dominique sat and placed her purse on her lap.

"You're looking fabulous as always."

"Thank you. What is this all about? Why couldn't you talk to me on the phone?" she asked, getting right to the point.

He chuckled. "You don't waste any time, do you." His expression sobered as he sat down. He looked directly across the table at her. "I want to talk to you about your career."

"What about it?"

"How can I put this?" He ran his hand through is thick black hair. "Dominique, the industry is changing."

Her pulse started to rise.

"The industry is looking for young fresh faces."

"What are you telling me?"

"I've had my feelers out—for months. All the roles that I know you would be ideal for are just not happening. Now of course if you'd gotten that Oscar nomination or won the Golden Globe we'd have more bargaining chips. But even that wasn't a guarantee. Look at Halle Berry. Since she won the Oscar for *Monster's Ball,* the only thing she's done is play a superhero and do makeup commercials."

A sick sensation settled in her stomach. She swallowed down the bile that rose to the back of her throat.

"What I'm saying is, folks aren't returning my calls when it comes to you." He put on his most earnest expression. "And believe me I've tried."

"I'm too old?" she asked incredulously. "I'm thirty-five for Christ's sake." Her eyes roamed the room searching for someplace to land.

He held up his hand. "I know. I know."

"Meryl Streep, Susan Sarandon, Diane Keaton… They're all nearly twice my age and still working."

Manny linked his fingers together on top of the

desk. He blew out a breath. "Think about how many black actresses you know of that get any major roles."

She was silent.

"Then factor in age." He looked at her for a long moment. "Now you get the picture? There's nothing out there."

"Nothing but those shit scripts I've been getting, you mean." Her grip tightened on her Kate Spade purse.

He blushed crimson. "I'm sorry, Dominique. We've hit a dry spell. I'm sure something will open up soon. We need to be patient." He turned on the charm. "I'm your biggest cheerleader. If it's out there, I'll get it. But I wanted you to hear it from me."

Her throat was clenched so tight she could barely swallow. When she tried to speak she began to cough.

Manny quickly poured her a glass of water and handed it to her. She took it with a shaky hand and gulped it down. She drew in a long breath.

"Any other good news you want to share with me today?"

"Don't kill the messenger."

She smiled sheepishly. "I'm sorry. I know you're trying. It's just so…unfair. I'm as good if not better than some of them out there."

"You'll get your shot. I know it."

"But in the meantime, be patient," she said, dripping sarcasm.

He nodded slowly, his mouth in a tight pink line. "Yes, just be patient."

She pushed herself to a standing position. "Thanks for telling me to my face."

He came from behind his desk and took her hand. "You're good, damned good. Don't forget that. I'll keep working and we'll get you working in a role you deserve. Promise." He walked her to the door and opened it. "I'll call the instant I hear anything."

She nodded, feeling numb, and passed Doris without a word as she walked out.

Manny watched her until she reached the elevator. He hated making promises he couldn't keep. He turned and closed his office door.

Dominique got behind the wheel of her Mercedes and slowly pulled out of the parking lot. As sad as it was, she knew Manny was right. Good roles for black actors were scarce, especially black women. Men had a much better shot and the screen seemed to love older men in general. The industry kept the doors wide open for men of any age. Women…were washed up for the most part after thirty. Maybe she should consider herself lucky to have lasted this long.

She eased out into traffic and merged with the slow-moving midday traffic of downtown Los Angeles. If she didn't act, what would she do? Her years of modeling were certainly over and she had no intention of walking down a runway in her under-wear. Television was an option, she supposed, some sitcom or other. There were no dramatic roles out there, either.

The more she thought about it the more depressed she became. She had to think of something. Acting was her life. She'd sacrificed so much to get where she was. She'd sacrificed her education, her family, friends, even having children of her own, all for the sake of her career. A career that was kicking her to the curb without a backward glance. She couldn't even say she had her marriage to fall back on. That, too, had begun to deteriorate.

When she returned home, Clifton was in the office. She could hear his raised voice from the foyer. She put down her purse and went to see what was wrong.

"Listen, Kristin or Kaitlyn or whatever your name is, you tell Winston that I expect a call back today!" He slammed down the phone then looked up and saw Dominique standing in the doorway with her mouth partly opened.

"That wasn't Winston Pierce's office, was it?" Winston Pierce was the new head of Longstreet Studios, one of the biggest in Hollywood.

Clifton clenched his jaw. "Yes," he bit out.

She entered the room. "Why in the world were you yelling like that?"

"Why? You wanna know why?" He pushed up from the swivel chair so hard it went scurrying across the room, banging against the far wall. "I've been calling his office for two weeks. Two weeks." He held up two fingers for emphasis. "And he hasn't bothered to return one phone call. Not one."

Rumor had it that Winston Pierce was ready to cast his next big picture for a script written by Stephen Sellers, one of the hottest producer-directors in the business. A role in that film would put her back where she rightfully belonged. Then her conversation with Manny came screaming back.

"Maybe Manny can call."

Clifton glared at her. "Manny has tried to call." His point was crystal clear.

Dominique lifted her chin ever so slightly. "He'll call back."

Clifton walked over to the desk and started sifting through papers. "Lions Gate, Warner Bros. Studios, DreamWorks. I've tried them all." He walked toward the window and looked out, sliding his hands into his pockets. "None of them have called back or, if they did, I was politely informed that nothing is available right now."

A sick sensation churned in her stomach.

Clifton lowered his head. She could hear his deep sigh from across the room. Slowly, she approached and stood behind him.

"Something will come along. I'm not worried," she said, forcing as much cheer as reasonable into her voice.

Clifton turned around. A soft smile framed his mouth. "This business is like a woman, temperamental."

She rested her head on his chest. He held her close. This is what she needed, she thought as she listened to the steady beat of her husband's heart. She needed to be held and told that, no matter what, they had each other.

"We have the whole house to ourselves," Clifton said into the softness of her hair.

She arched her neck and looked up into his eyes. They'd darkened with desire, a look she hadn't seen in far too long.

"The whole house?" she repeated coyly.

He stroked her back. "Yep."

"Then why don't we start upstairs and work our way down?"

"How 'bout we start right here and work our way up?" He lowered his head and kissed her tenderly on the mouth. Clifton pulled her close, the lines of their bodies melding. He unfastened the hook in the back of her pants and unzipped them. The soft fabric fell silently to the floor.

Dominique sighed softly as his hands wandered along the curves of her body. She pressed closer, needing to feel all of him. Yet even as she did, the emotional fulfillment she sought wouldn't come. It was as if her body and her spirit couldn't connect. It wasn't Clifton's tongue that searched out the heat of her mouth or his hands that sought to awaken that spot inside of her waiting to explode—it wasn't Clifton, it was Alan—and the realization terrified her.

# Chapter 6

The days turned into weeks, the weeks into months without a single script coming her way. Day after day, Dominique waited for "the call" that never came. It was wearing on her and Clifton had become surlier than usual.

"You look a mess," he groused, passing her in the hallway.

The sudden sting stopped her in her tracks. She glanced down at her casual outfit, which she felt was perfectly fine for staying indoors.

"What's wrong with what I have on?"

"You're putting on weight. That certainly isn't

going to help your situation," he said instead of responding to her question.

"Putting on weight? I haven't gained any weight."

"When's the last time you looked in the mirror?" He continued along the hallway and down the staircase.

Dominique went into her dressing room, snatched open the closet door that held a full-length mirror and looked at herself from every angle. Maybe she had gained a pound or two but nothing significant.

She heard the front door open then slam shut and moments later the sound of Clifton's car pulling out of the driveway. She didn't know if she was disappointed or relieved that he was gone. They'd done nothing but argue or, worse, cast stony silences in each other's direction for the past few weeks. Clifton placed all the blame for the lull in her career at her feet. He said she was too picky, then not picky enough. She could work if she really wanted to, but all she really wanted to do was to lay around and feel sorry for herself. He didn't like how she was keeping her hair, her nails were too long, then too short. She needed some sun, then she was too dark. Day after day the berating went on, followed by him storming out of the house for hours. She was a mental and emotional wreck, on a constant roller coaster. She'd begun to dread the sound of his car pulling into the driveway or to hear his voice in the house. She felt like a prisoner in her own home.

She stared at her reflection.

Maybe weight was an issue, she thought dismally.

Everyone was so rail-thin these days. Perhaps that was one of the reasons for her not getting any new offers. Film and television added ten pounds. She sucked in her already flat stomach and tucked in her round rear. First thing tomorrow she would go to the gym.

There was a light knock on her bedroom door.

"Yes?"

"I've prepared lunch out on the patio," Marcia said.

"Oh, thank you. I'll be down."

"Will Mr. Burrell be joining you?"

"Um, no. He had to go out. Business."

Marcia looked at her for a moment before nodding her head and walking out.

Dominique tried to ascertain the look Marcia had given her before she left but couldn't put her finger on it, although it appeared to border on disbelief. She shook it off and went downstairs and out to the patio.

As Marcia had said, the table was set beneath the umbrella: fresh salad, grilled chicken strips on a bed of saffron rice, a carafe of iced tea and a bottle of white wine, complete with white linen napkins and her outdoor china and flatware. A bud vase with a single yellow rose sat in the center.

Dominique looked at the elegantly set table and inhaled the savory aroma. Her stomach growled with hunger. But then she remembered what Clifton had said. She reached for the bottle of wine, used the corkscrew to open it and poured a glass.

She sat down and took a thoughtful sip, then

another. She eyed the food, but took another swallow of wine instead.

She glanced across the table and noticed the new edition of *Variety* folded neatly. She picked it up and began flipping through the pages, stopping cold when she saw a picture of Alan Conners. Her heart kicked up a notch then beat in a steady racing rhythm along with the driving pulse between her thighs.

It was an innocent enough picture. It was a photograph of him being interviewed at one of the studios in downtown L.A. He was casually dressed in a pair of faded jeans and a black T-shirt that hugged his upper body like a long lost lover. Her face grew warm. This image of him was in such contrast to the times when she'd seen him in formal settings. Here, he appeared even more appealing, the raw sexuality of him leaping off the page. The article went on to say that he would be returning to Atlanta to consider some new projects but that his current venture was to launch his own production company with his brother-in-law, which they hoped to get up and running by the end of the year.

She put the magazine down, but didn't take her eyes off Alan's picture. Why was she so drawn to him? It was unnerving. Even that night, weeks ago when she and Clifton had made love for the first time in ages, her mind and her body had been consumed by images of Alan Conners. She imagined his hands on her breasts, between her legs. It was him that filled her, not her husband.

When the act between her and Clifton was over, she felt so ashamed, as if she'd actually cheated on her husband. But the fantasy of being made love to by Alan wouldn't leave her. So much so that even the times when she pleased herself, she imagined that it was him. It was making her crazy. And when she looked at her husband she could swear that he could read her adulterous thoughts.

She reached for her wineglass, brought it to her lips and emptied it, then quickly refilled it. By the time she finally got up from the table, the world was slightly askew. She giggled. Life wasn't so bad. So what if she didn't have a job and she was a has-been at thirty-five. So what if she had a husband that she couldn't make love to without thinking of another man. So what if she didn't really have any friends or family. Big deal. She was Dominique Laws, movie star with a big-ass house in Beverly Hills and a slew of some good and some bad movies in her repertoire. She had money, cars and plenty of clothes. What else could a person want, anyway? She grabbed the magazine and held it close to her chest then pushed away from the table, stumbling slightly. The empty bottle rocked then tipped over. Dominique giggled, opened the sliding glass doors of the patio and went back inside.

Marcia watched her employer's progress from the vantage point of the kitchen doorway. She pursed her lips and slowly shook her head before turning back to finish her chores.

Dominique managed to get upstairs and as soon as she did, she tumbled across her bed. Her head pounded and the room swayed every time she moved her head. She chuckled but it wasn't because she found anything even moderately amusing. Rather, she chuckled at what she and her life had become.

When she'd met Clifton she'd gravitated to him for so many reasons. Not necessarily because of what he told her he could do for her, but because he was the mature male figure she'd never had. Clifton Burrell was the first *real* man in her life. She'd never had the luxury of sitting on her dad's lap and finding out the ways of the world, being told how to be treated by a man, what she should expect. Her father, whoever he was, didn't exist in her life. Her mother, God rest her soul, was a common hooker. It was her sister Annette who had taken care of her, although Annette resented every minute of it and didn't fail to mention it to Dominique every chance she got.

"You the reason why Daddy left in the first place," she would say while she braided Dominique's long black hair. "And you the reason why Mama gotta turn tricks to keep the lights on. When you came everything changed."

Dominique carried around that guilt like an extra limb. It was with her everywhere, in everything she did, her every thought.

So when she met Clifton and he showed her that

he cared as much about her as he did about making her a star, what else could she do but fall for him?

That was fifteen years ago. So much had changed. She still cared for Clifton. He'd made her into a household name. He'd taught her everything and what he couldn't teach her, he got someone else to. He did everything for her. He managed her career, took care of all the bills, put himself between her and those that stood in her way. But did she still love him? Did she ever love him? Or was what she'd been feeling all these years no more than gratitude coupled with lust?

The questions along with the dark images of her past churned and churned in her head until she finally drifted off into a dreamless sleep.

The sound of voices in the distance floated to her. Slowly she opened her eyes. The room was entirely dark. She tried to sit up, her head throbbing with the effort. She lay back down and tried to piece together why the room was so dark. Gingerly, she turned her head toward the window. Stars hung in the sky. She frowned then looked at the digital clock on the nightstand. It was nearly ten.

How could that be? She'd slept for hours. The last thing she remembered was coming upstairs. She trudged through the sludge of her brain trying to think about what happened. In bits and pieces it came back to her. She closed her eyes. She'd knocked off a whole bottle of wine on an empty stomach.

By degrees she sat up. Something rustled

beneath her. She reached behind her. It was the magazine. She'd actually fallen to sleep holding the picture of Alan in her hand. A pang of guilt knotted her stomach.

Someone was on the stairs. Moments later Clifton's figure filled the doorway of their bedroom. He flicked on the lights and stood glaring at her. Dominique squinted against the glare.

"You're finally up," he said sarcastically. "We have company. It would be nice if you could get yourself together and join us."

She couldn't think straight. The way she was feeling it would take her hours to pull herself together.

"Who's here?" she said, her voice thick and scratchy.

"Justin Forman. He has a screenplay that he's been shopping around. I think you would be perfect for the part. I want you to meet him and make a good impression." He stood there for a moment more. "And hurry up." He whirled away and returned downstairs.

Moments later conversation floated up to her.

Dominique covered her face with her hands. She had to get it together. Maybe this was the opportunity she'd been waiting for. Although she'd never heard of Justin Forman, that didn't mean it wasn't a brilliant script.

She drew in a long breath to try to clear her head and settle her stomach before getting up and heading into the bathroom. A quick shower would certainly help.

In less than a half hour, Dominique joined her husband, still feeling a bit wobbly, but able to pull it off. She was an actress.

Dominique put on her best ready-for-my-close-up smile and walked into the room. Both men stood up. "I thought I'd give you gentleman plenty of time to talk before I barged in," she said. She extended her hand to Justin, who looked to be about twenty-one and counting. He still had the pink blush of youth in his face.

"Pleasure to meet you, Ms. Laws. I'm a big fan of your work."

Her brows arched. "Really. Thank you. Glad you enjoy my work." She turned to Clifton, placing a hand on his arm. "Can I get you anything, sweetheart?"

"You can refresh this brandy." He handed her his empty glass.

"Sure." She turned to Justin. "Can I get you anything, Justin?"

He waved his hand. "No, thanks. I'm good."

Dominique wandered over to the bar and replenished Clifton's drink then decided to fix one for herself. It would help to calm her nerves. She returned to the seating area and eased down next to Clifton, handing him his drink.

"Justin was telling me about his screenplay," Clifton said.

Dominique turned her attention to Justin. "What is it about?"

"Well…" He told her about his idea for a comedy centered around a high school in which she would have a small role as a teacher.

"I see," she said, but didn't. How could Clifton think this was something for her? She gave him a tight smile.

"Of course there is a possibility that the role could develop into something more, but that's the way I see it now," he continued.

"We'd be happy to look over the script," Clifton said. Dominique flashed him a look that Justin missed while he was digging in his leather satchel for a copy of the script.

He handed the script to Clifton.

"I know this isn't something you generally do, Ms. Laws, but my goal is that by attaching your name to the project I could get the interest of a director." He smiled hopefully.

Dominique finished off her drink, slowly rose and went to refill her glass. She returned to the couch. "I will certainly take a look at it. I appreciate you thinking of me. Um, is this your first script?"

"Yes." He bobbed his head. "It's good. I've been working on it for a while and I know in the right hands it can really be something."

Why did she get out of bed? "Of course."

"Have you shown the script around?" Clifton asked.

Justin's hopeful expression sank. "Yes. It's been a struggle."

"This is a tough town," Dominique said absently. She stared out the window and sipped on her drink until she'd drained the glass.

Clifton and Justin continued talking without her. This was all so wrong, she thought. And what was worst was that Clifton acted as if this was some golden opportunity. Maybe it would be if she were just starting out in the business. But she wasn't.

When she looked up, Justin was putting his belongings together.

"It's really been a thrill to meet you, Ms. Laws. I hope you will consider signing on to this project."

She shook his hand. "Thanks again for stopping by."

Clifton walked him to the door and returned shortly. His caramel-toned face was livid.

"What the hell is wrong with you?"

"With me? What the hell is wrong with you? Why in the world would you even entertain something like that?"

He cupped his palm to his ear. "Do you hear that?"

"Hear what?"

"Someone knocking on the door?"

Her expression tightened.

"Right, neither do I. No one is knocking, Nikki. Not a damned soul.

"Even when I was just starting out you wouldn't think of asking me to do something like this or any of the others that have come our way lately."

"Maybe that was because you weren't a has-been

before." He threw a nasty look in her direction before storming off.

Dominique's chest caved in as if all the wind had been kicked out of her. *Has-been.* Is that what she was? Is that what he believed?

She walked over to the bar and took the bottle of brandy and a glass and went out to the patio.

That's where Marcia found her the following morning, slumped over the table, with the empty bottle turned over on its side.

Marcia stood over Dominique for several moments. The smell of old liquor wafted around her. Rich people, she thought. They had no idea what struggle really was so the minute things didn't go their way they fall apart. She snorted in disgust.

Although Dominique was always pleasant to her, she was no different from all the others: a closet full of expensive clothes, boxes filled with jewelry, cars, people waiting on you hand and foot. She picked up the empty bottle and held it up to the light. The cost of this one bottle could feed her family. She set it back down on the table. The right thing to do would be to wake the missus up. How could her husband not have noticed that she hadn't come to bed all night? Then it hit her. Maybe he did and didn't care. She knew that things were strained between the two of them and had been for months now.

Marcia studied Dominique's profile. In the light of day she was as ordinary as the next woman. All she did was get a break. That's all Marcia needed was a break and she'd never have to work as someone's maid ever again.

She set the empty bottle back down on the table and walked away.

The glare from the sun burned behind Dominique's closed lids and warmed her face. She stirred. Every bone in her body ached. Gradually, she dared open her eyes and was stunned to see her surroundings.

She lifted her head up from the fold of her arms and glanced around. She had on the same clothes from the night before. The empty bottle of brandy stood in accusation.

She rubbed her eyes and sat up. Her stomach revolted. She moaned. What the hell had happened? Had she actually passed out?

With great effort she stood, rocked for a second or two, then righted herself. She shook her head to clear it and made her way inside. The house was quiet. She tiptoed upstairs praying not to run into Marcia on the way. Each step seemed to vibrate through her entire body then settle in her head with a dull unrelenting throb.

She got to her bedroom and found it empty. Clifton was probably gone. He generally was lately. Why hadn't he come to look for her all night? She glanced at the bed. It hadn't been touched. He hadn't spent the night here.

She went into the bathroom, opened the medicine cabinet and took out a bottle of aspirin. She shook two into her palm then turned on the faucet. She scooped handfuls of water into her mouth, tossed the aspirin to the back of her throat and swallowed.

It was the beginning of a downward spiral.

*Chapter 7*

It was more than a month later when the phone stirred Dominique out of a stupor. The only thing that helped her sleep alone every night was a glass or two or three of brandy. A bottle of wine in the morning took the edge off her hangover.

Clifton had become more and more of a ghost and Marcia merely looked at her with an arched brow. All she had was herself and her bottle, which was fine with her.

The phone jangled again. It seemed louder this time. Dominique groaned and turned over. Still with her eyes shut she reached for the phone.

"Hello," she said, her voice thick and slurred.

"Dominique, is that you?"

"Who else were you expecting?" Her head pounded.

"This is Manny. I have an audition for you."

Her tongue felt woolly and heavy. "A what?"

"An audition. Are you all right? You sound...drunk."

She giggled and that set off the marching band in her head. She squeezed her eyes shut and massaged her temple with her free hand. "Don't be silly. I was just resting."

"At three o'clock in the afternoon?"

"Is that why you called—to see what I was doing?"

She heard his long sigh.

"Look, I have an audition for you for tomorrow morning at ten. It's for a *CoverGirl* commercial. The pay is great and you'll get national exposure as well as spreads in all the major magazines."

Her head jerked back. "Commercial?"

"This is an opportunity. All of the stars are doing them."

"Stars," she said in a childlike voice. "You think I'm a star, Manny? No one else does."

"Dominique, whatever is going on, you need to pull yourself together. Don't blow this off. I had to kick ass and take names to get this audition for you."

"Okay. Okay. Where do I have to go?"

He gave her all the details. "I'll also e-mail you so you'll have the info."

"Thanks." Her head dropped back down on the pillow.

"And give Evelyn a call. She's been bugging me to get you on some kind of committee thing she's working on."

"I will. Promise."

"Good. And break a leg tomorrow."

She hung up the phone. Commercial audition…well if it was good enough for Halle and Queen Latifah and Nicole Kidman, it was good enough for her.

She could get herself together. She could. Forcing herself, she rolled off the bed and made it to a standing position. She stumbled into the bathroom and looked at herself in the mirror.

Dark circles hung around bloodshot eyes. Her face looked puffy and her hair like a bird's nest. She took a comb and tugged it through the tangles, wincing with every pull.

She began to weep.

By the time Clifton arrived home that evening she had pulled herself into a sufficiently decent state. She'd gone to the salon earlier to have her hair and nails done and had been resting with cucumbers on her eyelids hoping to reduce the swelling and sagging until shortly before Clifton came in.

"Well, at least you're not passed out somewhere," he greeted her. "Should I be happy or simply wait for the inevitable?"

She drew herself up. "Manny called today. He has an audition for me for tomorrow."

He seemed interested. "For what?"

"A commercial," she said meekly.

"Commercial! You're kidding right?"

"No. It's major."

"You wouldn't take the roles that were offered to you, but you'd do a commercial."

"All the actors are doing them. Manny said so."

He looked at her as if she'd sprouted two heads. "You want to do this then go ahead. It's all downhill from there." He walked out.

How much further downhill could she go? She'd been pretty much shunned by an industry she'd given years of her life to. Her husband barely looked at her. What else was there? She turned and the wet bar called out to her. What the hell, she figured, and fixed herself a drink.


The next thing she remembered was being sprawled out on the bed with the phone shrilling in the background. She opened one eye and squinted into the blazing morning sunshine. She peered at the digital clock. Nine-thirty. She moaned. There was something she was supposed to do today. The phone rang and rang. Finally she grabbed it and garbled out a hello.

"Dominique! I called the casting office to confirm your appointment and they said you hadn't arrived yet. I called your cell, no answer. What are you still doing at home?"

She pushed up on her elbows and worked hard

trying to put the pieces together. Casting office…
Manny on the phone…confirm appointment. Her
heart immediately started to race. Oh, my God. She
jerked up in the bed looking wildly around.

"Manny…I, um, was just darting out of the door."

"What? It's a forty-five minute drive when there's
no traffic."

She breathed in and out to calm herself. "I know,
I…"

"Dominique there are no second chances with
this one, either you show up or you blow it. Those
are the choices."

Her head was pounding so badly she couldn't think.

"I'll call Carol the casting director and let her
know that you had a minor fender bender. You're
fine, but you need to move your time up about an
hour and a half. Can you get there by eleven-thirty?"

"Yes, definitely." She brushed her hair out of her
face. "I'll be there."

"Don't screw this up, Dom."

"I won't, I promise."

The instant she got off the phone she walked as
fast as her pounding head would allow into the
bathroom. She turned on the shower full-blast and
stepped in beneath the beating cool water. Soon her
head began to clear. She took two aspirin, straight,
dried off and looked for something to wear.

Sitting in front of her dressing table mirror she at-
tempted to apply her makeup. But her hands shook

so badly it was an exercise in futility. The best she could do was apply some foundation in the hopes of hiding her now dry and sallow skin and the shadows beneath her eyes that hung like clouds before a storm.

She put on the outfit that she'd selected. It was one of her favorite designer suits. But when she tried to zip the pants it wouldn't budge. She held in her stomach and tugged until she nearly passed out from holding her breath. Finally she got the zipper up and was appalled to see her stomach slightly protruding over the top of the waistband.

A line of perspiration broke out across her forehead. The jacket would hide all that, she decided. She simply wouldn't take it off.

She ran her hand across her hair. The beautiful style she'd had yesterday was gone. The curls had lost their bounce and hung limply around her head. Quickly she gathered her hair up and twisted it into a loose knot on top of her head, letting a few strands linger around the sides of her face.

Mollified, she took one last look, grabbed her purse and car keys and rushed out.

"Oh, Ms. Laws, I didn't realize you were up."

"Yes, I have an appointment. I'm already running late." She hurried toward the door, her heels clicking rapidly against the marble tiles.

"Will you be back for dinner?"

"Yes, but don't fuss over anything. I know I'll be gone a few hours, maybe longer." She rushed out.

On the drive over she was a nervous wreck and was a breath away from rear-ending a soccer mom and her brood. Every few minutes she kept checking the car's clock. That only brought on more anxiety. The time seemed to be flying by and traffic was crawling.

By the time she arrived at the building where the casting offices were, her back was soaking wet and she was shaky all over. Her stomach was doing backflips.

Dominique got to the elevator and studied the board above for the floor. The doors swished open and a herd of people poured off. She managed to sidestep everyone and get on. She pressed eighteen.

On the ride up she tried to will herself to be calm. She'd done a zillion auditions. It was no big deal. But back then, the offers came so fast and furious that she had to turn down more than she could take on. Now it was the other way around. She was begging for a chance and she'd swear she could smell her own desperation.

The elevator stopped on the eighteenth floor. She stepped out onto a carpeted hallway. The stark white walls made the narrow hall seem much larger than it actually was. Stainless steel signs with engraved lettering gave directions to various offices. Carol Masters Casting was to the left, room 1878.

She moved silently down the hallway, her footfalls and pounding heartbeat muffled by the carpet. 1878 was the next door. She turned the gold knob and stepped in.

A receptionist with a headset hooked to her ear looked up. "Good afternoon. How can I help you?"

"I have an audition with…for the CoverGirl commercial."

The redhead looked Dominique over as she handed her the sign-in log. "Name?"

"Dominique Laws."

The receptionist spun her chair to face the computer screen, made a few quick key strokes then turned her green eyes to Dominique. "Your appointment was for ten."

"I know. Um, my agent said he was going to call. I had an accident…car accident. That's why I'm late."

The woman's lips pinched. "I just came on about twenty minutes ago. Maybe Reese took the message. But I don't have any notes here." She blew out a sigh. "Let me check and find out if they can still see you." She punched some numbers into the phone and flipped the sign-in log around so that she could read it.

"Yeah, Tracy, there's a Dominique Laws here for the commercial. She had a ten o'clock. Hmm, okay. Sure." She disconnected the call. "They'll see you in about five minutes. You can wait over there." She pointed to a long leather bench that butted the wall.

Dominique went to sit down, thankful to get off her shaky legs. She squeezed her purse between her fingers and pressed her knees together.

A spunky brunette with long stringy hair poked her head out of the door. "Dominique," she called out.

Dominique stood up and approached.

"Hi, I'm Tracy." She held the door for Dominique. "Right this way. It's been a busy morning," she said practically jogging. "Done many of these?"

"Excuse me?" Dominique said, a bit breathlessly.

"Auditions. Have you done many of them?"

If the question weren't so painfully sad she would laugh at the absurdity of it. They truly had no clue who she was or what she'd done. It was a brand-new generation with fresh faces and short memories. "Yes, quite a few, actually."

"Good then I don't have to tell you not to be nervous." She opened another door. "Right inside. Good luck."

Dominique stepped into a small room with a single camera, four men and one woman sat in chairs.

The woman was the first to acknowledge her presence. "Dominique?"

"Yes."

The woman approached. "Carol Masters. Sorry to hear about your accident this morning. I would have rescheduled, but this is the last day. You do understand."

"Sure. Not a problem." She swallowed over the hard knot in her throat.

"Glen, pass me the script." She took the script from the assistant and handed it to Dominique. "Real simple and straightforward. Read the lines, look into the camera."

Dominique nodded.

Carol returned to her seat and the cameraman got behind the camera.

"Ready when you are, Dominique."

Dominique looked at the script and the words began to blur and run together. She blinked several times to clear her vision.

"There's… This is a face without CoverGirl." She looked into the camera. The directions said to flash a broad energetic smile. She tried. "Here is a Cover-Girl face."

Carol looked at the other men seated. Their expressions went from bland to disinterested. "How 'bout one more time, Dominique?"

She drew in a breath.

"From the top," one of the men directed. "And see if you can put a little emotion in it."

Dominique nodded, stared at the script then read the lines. Her voice sound unnatural to her ears.

"Okay. Thanks for coming."

Dominique dropped the script to her side and stood there.

"Thanks for coming," Carol said.

"Did I get the part?"

"Um, we'll give your agent a call."

Dominique started to laugh. "You'll call my agent? Don't pull my chain. You're not going to call. No one calls!" Her voice rose exponentially. She threw the script across the room catching one of the men on the side of the head. He leapt up from his seat.

"Get her out of here."

"You're not going to call." Her face twisted in anguish and pent-up fury. She stormed back and forth across the room looking for something to throw. "You all lie. You lie all the time." She pulled at her hair. It fell in wild waves around her face.

Carol held her palms forward. "Just calm down," she said gently.

"Don't patronize me," she spat. "Don't you dare!" She kicked over a chair and continued stomping around the room.

"Somebody call security," one of the men shouted.

The young woman from the front desk came rushing in.

"Call security!" the man shouted.

The girl darted back out.

"Why do you all do this?" Dominique cried. "Why do you build us up to tear us down, toss us aside like garbage when you're done? Why? Why?"

Tears streamed down her face. Her nose was running and she wiped it with the back of her hand. She wanted to hurt something, somebody. Any way to share her pain and humiliation.

The door burst open and two large men in standard powder-blue shirts and dark blue pants marched in.

Dominique whirled toward them. "Don't touch me! Don't you dare touch me," she said from a half-crouched position.

"We can do this the easy way or the hard way, ma'am."

She turned red-rimmed eyes on the stunned casting staff. She sniffed hard. "You'll call? You promise you'll call?" she said in a tiny voice.

One of the guards took her by the arm and led her to the door. She didn't struggle. She was too tired.

They escorted her to the elevator and out of the building. Once outside, Dominique stood on the sidewalk. Pedestrians walked around her. Several jostled her but she didn't move. Gray clouds moved above the buildings, camouflaging the sun.

The first drop of rain hit her on her nose. The second on her lips. She tilted her head upward. The rain fell in soft steady droplets. Pedestrians walked faster. Dominique finally moved, started toward her car parked on the next street over. By the time she reached it she was soaked to the skin. She didn't care.

When she pulled off she knew she wasn't going home. She drove around in the rain until she found a bar.

By the time she arrived home, the buzz she had was worn off. She dropped her purse and car keys on the antique table that graced the foyer. All she wanted to do was take a hot bath and crawl back into bed. Images of the fool she'd made of herself during the audition kept jumping out in front of her like a kid trying to scare an unsuspecting victim. She didn't want to think about what Manny would say when he found out.

The house was quiet. Marcia must have gone home for the day, she concluded. She climbed the stairs and walked down the hallway toward her bedroom. When she opened her bedroom door, her blood went cold. She couldn't move. And neither did they.

Clifton was in the throes of sex with Marcia. Her soft moans of delight filled the room. He must have sensed Dominique watching. He glanced over his shoulder but never missed a beat and went back to screwing Marcia as if Dominique didn't exist.

A wave of nausea rocked her stomach. She stumbled back, heaving, but not before slamming the door with a reverberating thud. Blindly, she ran down the hall to the stairs. She snatched up her purse and car keys and ran out into the rainy evening. Once behind the wheel she sat trembling. She stared up at the house through the rain, certain that any moment now, Clifton was going to come flying out the door to explain—tell her at the very least a lie. But he didn't.

Her insides ached with a kind of pain she couldn't put words to. *Clifton and Marcia*. The ugly cliché—your husband cheating with the housekeeper. In her house. In her bed. How long had it been going on?

What the hell did it matter? There was no explanation, no justification. And quite frankly, she didn't give a damn. Whatever fleeting hope she may have harbored about working things out with Clifton was gone.

Dominique put the car in gear and drove off.

# Chapter 8

"Clif, this is Manny. I've been calling for days. Where is Dominique?"

Clifton paced with the phone tucked between his shoulder and his ear. "She's not here right now."

"Where is she? Did she talk to you about what happened at the audition?"

"Um, no."

"Look, I don't know what's going on, but it ain't good. Security had to escort her out of there. I tried to smooth it over with Carol, but as far as she's concerned, she won't even think about casting Dominique again. Do you have any idea how hard it was for me to book that gig?"

"I'll talk to her."

"I don't think you're getting what I'm saying, Clif. Dominique is screwed. This fiasco is going to spread like wildfire in the industry. It's going to take more than a miracle and a high-priced PR agency to make this disappear."

"I'll talk to her," he repeated.

Manny blew out his frustration. "Have Dominique call me."

"Yeah, yeah. I will." He hung up.

He knew he should have never taken Manny's call. He'd been ducking him for nearly two weeks— as long as Dominique had been gone. He'd been sure that Dominique would have thrown some kind of fit when she found him in bed with Marcia. Instead, she'd simply walked out and hadn't been back since. He'd made discrete inquiries, but to date nothing had turned up. As much as he was reluctant to admit it, he was beginning to worry.

There was no way that he could get Manny off the scent once he'd gotten a whiff that something was wrong. Dominique was one of his prized clients, at least she had been. He wouldn't stop until he found her, wherever she was.

Clifton stepped out onto the patio and stared at the landscape beyond. All he wanted was out. He wasn't sure when he'd stopped loving Dominique or if he'd ever loved her. She was his project, someone young and impressionable that he could mold to his satisfaction. He'd created Dominique Laws and presented her to the world. They'd both reaped the benefits over the years. The farce of their marriage more than likely could have gone on indefinitely. Until Dominique's star began to fall and lose its shine.

Where was she?

Dominique sat on the hard wooden chair by the dusty window with her head in her hands. It pounded against her fingertips. Through bleary eyes, she looked out onto the alleyway just beyond her window. How long had she been here? Slowly she turned to take in her surroundings. The tiny room with the warped floors and peeling paint stood as a stark testimony to how far she had fallen.

Several empty liquor bottles sat on a rickety table alongside a plastic cup. A threadbare blanket covered a two-inch mattress. She supposed whatever was behind the door was a bathroom. She should feel ashamed, appalled, something, but she felt nothing, as if her insides had been carved out and a gaping hole was the only thing left. Maybe that was a good thing. Surely, if she was to feel anything at all it would be her own undoing.

She used the back of the chair to brace herself as she stood. Her legs didn't want to obey, but finally she was able to stand on her own and she shuffled like a woman three times her age to the bathroom.

The inside of it made her gag. Water dripped in the

rusty sink. The tub hadn't been cleaned in who knew how long and there was a foul odor coming from the toilet. Roaches had set up camp at the foot of the sink and refused to move even when she kicked at them.

Gingerly, she touched the knobs of the sink and turned on the water. It took several moments for the water to turn from a light brown to something that was reasonably clear. She didn't dare use the very off-white towel that hung on the rusty pole. Instead, she splashed the lukewarm water on her face and allowed it to air dry.

She lifted her head and glanced into the cracked mirror. The woman she saw was unrecognizable. Just as well, she thought miserably. She didn't want to know her. She turned away and returned to her new home, wherever that was.

She tried to remember how she'd gotten here, but couldn't. The last thing she remembered with any sort of clarity was running out of the house after seeing Clifton in bed with their housekeeper. She walked to the table and lifted one of the bottles. There was a thin line of liquor left in the bottom of the bottle. She lifted it to her lips and finished it off before slumping down onto the bed. She felt the springs jab her in the back.

She thought she remembered an audition. Slowly the debacle came back to her. She groaned. How long had she been here? What day was it? She fumbled for her purse that sat on the table next to the bottles. She took out her cell phone and saw it flashing, indicating that she had messages waiting. When she checked she had ten messages from Manny, each one more urgent than the last. There wasn't one from Clifton. Did she expect that there would be?

A pounding on the door drew her attention.

"Who is it?" she shouted in a ragged voice.

"Management. You owe for this week," came the voice in a thick Hispanic accent.

She blinked. *This week?* She got up from the bed and went to the door. When she opened it a series of flashbulbs went off in her face. Her hand flew to her eyes to cover them.

"Look this way, Ms. Laws."

"Over here!"

"Ms. Laws, why are you here?

"Is it drugs?"

Panic gripped her. She slammed the door. Her heart pounded in a crazy, erratic rhythm. She pressed her back to the door as the shouts from the other side continued demanding that she answer their questions.

"Oh God," she moaned. How did they find her? The only answer had to be the hotel clerk. Did she pay cash or with her credit card? She couldn't remember.

The panic rose. She had to get out of there. But she was sure reporters were camped out in front of the motel. Still she couldn't stay there indefinitely.

What was she going to do?

\* \* \*

"Mr. Breevort, there's a call for you on line two," his secretary said, sticking her head inside his office door. "It's a reporter. He says it's about Dominique."

He frowned with concern. "A reporter?" His pulse kicked up a notch. It couldn't be good whatever it was. He snatched up the phone. "Who is this?"

"Mr. Breevort. Are you Dominique Laws's agent?"

"Who is this?"

"I'm a reporter from *The Star.*"

Manny shut his eyes and silently groaned. The tabloids were the worst. It was probably about the aborted audition.

"What do you want?"

"I wanted to hear your comments about Ms. Laws being holed up in a motel in South Central L.A. We do have photographs and I wanted to get any comments from you before we went to press."

Manny mouth dropped open. Think, man, think. "You must be wrong."

"Pictures don't lie."

"No, but reporters do. What proof do I have that you're telling me the truth?"

"I'll e-mail you the pictures. Then you tell me how wrong I am."

"Fine. Here's my e-mail address."

"They're on their way. Then I'll call back. My deadline is five."

Manny hung up the phone and swung his chair

toward his computer. He surfed over to his e-mail account and waited. In moments, a notice that he had new mail appeared. He clicked on the file and downloaded the contents. There were three photos, one worse than the next, all of them of Dominique.

His stomach twisted into a knot. Did Clifton know? If he did, he hadn't seen fit to tell him anything or even mention the fact that Dominique was gone.

Line two flashed. He didn't wait for his secretary to answer.

"Yes," he barked into the phone.

"Well?"

"Where were these pictures taken?"

"At the Primrose Motel on Valley about an hour ago."

Manny swallowed over the lump in his throat. "Look, how much is it going to cost me to bury those pictures?"

"Now, Mr. Breevort, that's unethical. Besides, I'm not the only reporter with these photos."

Manny cringed. "Dominique is practicing for a role. As you know she researches all her characters. It's all very hush-hush."

"So you're telling me that this is all part of rehearsal?" He laughed at the absurdity. "Well, I'll be sure to include your comments in the article." He hung up before Manny could say another word.

Manny sat there with his hand still on the phone. This went beyond damage control. Once those photos hit the newsstand there wasn't much recovery from that. It would only be a matter of time before the major publications picked up on it.

He pressed the intercom.

"Yes, Mr. Breevort?"

"Have my car brought around."

"Yes, sir."

He got his jacket and rushed out. "I'll be gone for the rest of the day," he said to his stunned secretary as he breezed past her and headed for the elevator.

Manny gripped the steering wheel as he sat in the bumper-to-bumper traffic on the freeway. She was clear on the other side of town, a part of town he wouldn't normally venture into even in broad daylight.

As he moved out of a downtown L.A., the landscape began to change. The homes went from grand to mid-range to a variety of two- to three-story abodes. Groups of men and women hung on corners; burned-out buildings peppered the streets.

More than an hour after leaving his office he found Valley. Was it left or right? He eased out into the intersection and looked both ways. To his right looked like more worn-out housing. To the left looked more like a commercial strip. He turned left. About eight blocks down, the flickering light of the Primrose Motel flashed against the waning light.

At least he didn't see any signs of reporters lurking around. He pulled into the driveway, got out and pushed through the swinging glass door.

A sweaty overweight man sat behind a worn wooden desk.

"Can I help you?"

Manny took off his sunglasses. The place reeked of old and ugly. He felt like brushing off his clothing.

"I'm looking for a woman." He took out a photo of Dominique.

The man's dull eyes brightened. "Oh, yes. Plenty people came to see her today." He grinned flashing a row of brown teeth.

"Can you tell me if she's still here?"

"Hasn't been out of that room since she come. Two weeks now. Except to ask for more of something to drink." He grinned again. "I usually send my daughter to get it for her."

This was as bad as he'd thought. "Okay. Can you take me to her room please?"

"You a friend? Husband?"

"Friend."

He looked Manny over for a moment. "Okay. Room 23. At the top of the stairs on your right."

It was apparent that there were no privacy rules at the Primrose.

Manny nodded his thanks and walked down the dank hallway then up the stairs. Room 23 was in front of him. He had no idea what to expect, but it couldn't be any worse than the pictures he'd seen. He approached the door, hesitated a second, then knocked.

"Go away!"

"Dom, it's me, Manny."

"Liar. Go away."

"Dominique, open the door. It's Manny. I want to help you, sweetheart." He heard soft sobs coming from the other side of the door.

"Dominique, come on, honey, let me in. It's going to be all right. I promise."

He heard movement and then the soft click of the lock disengaging. Slowly the door eased back. His breath caught and his heart literally ached when he saw her. This was not the woman he knew.

She lowered her head, unable to meet the sadness and disappointment in his eyes.

Manny came in and quickly shut the door behind her. Dominique stumbled away and went to sit on the side of the bed.

Manny looked around at the squalor but most of all at the mess that had become Dominique.

"Dominique," he began gently, "talk to me. What is going on?"

She shook her head, her wild hair swinging around her face. "It's over."

"What is?"

"Everything. My career, my marriage." She turned bloodshot eyes on him. Water hung on her lower lids. "Photographers were here today." Her voice broke into tiny pieces. "They saw me. They took pictures."

Manny slid closer and put his arm around her

shoulder. "It's going to be okay. We're going to get you out of here."

"I have nowhere to go. Can't go home. I won't."

"I know you don't mean that. Clif will want to know that you're okay."

She jumped up with surprising agility before wobbling on her feet. "He doesn't give a damn about me! He's screwing the help." She tossed her head back and laughed and laughed, the sound bordering on hysteria.

Manny got up, grabbed her by the shoulders and shook her. "Stop it. Look at me. I don't know what happened with Clifton and quite frankly nothing he would do could surprise me. But the bottom line is you need help, Dominique." He looked at the lineup of empty liquor bottles.

She focused on him, her eyes wide. "You'll help me?"

He nodded. "Anything you need. But first we have to get you out of this place."

"They're out there," she said, panic rising the octave of her voice. "They'll take more pictures." She covered her face.

"No one is out there. They're all gone. It's just me and you."

Her bottom lip trembled. "Promise?"

"Promise." He looked around. "Let me help you get your things." He picked up her jacket from the back of the chair and her purse from the table. He helped her put on her shoes. "Come on, sweetie, lean on me. Let's get out of here."

She nodded her head against his side and allowed him to lead her out.


"What in the world happened to her?" Evelyn whispered to her husband as they shut the door to the guest bedroom. Her soft expression was a series of worry lines.

"I'll tell you what I know downstairs."

They went down to the kitchen and sat down. Manny began telling her how he'd finally found out where Dominique was and what he was sure would be the major scandal that would ensue once the papers hit the stands.

"My God. But why? When we last saw her she looked fine. She seemed fine, maybe a bit distracted, but fine."

"She's a very good actress," he said tongue in cheek. "She let us see what she wanted us to see." He paused. "There's more."

Evelyn sat with her mouth open when Manny told her about Clifton and Marcia.

"That bastard. And he knew she'd seen them?"

"Appears so, according to Dominique."

Evelyn shook her head. "So what are you planning to do? She can't stay here indefinitely."

"I know, but Dominique needs help. She needs to dry out. She needs someone to talk to and she probably needs a good divorce lawyer."

## Chapter 9

Marcia brought the papers to the kitchen table and dropped them in front of Clifton.

"You see this?"

Clifton snatched up the paper. A picture of Dominique looking wild and unkempt was on the front page of *The Star* and *The Globe*. He flipped through and found the article. The more he read, the more irate he became. The fool, he thought. She was always weak. What was she thinking? He tossed the paper aside.

"What are you going to do?"

Clifton looked at Marcia. "Do about what?"

"About your wife?"

"My wife seems to be handling things on her own." He got up from the table. "I'm going out. When I get back, I'll expect that you'll be gone."

"What!"

"Gone. There's a check for you on the table in the hall. It should cover any issues you might have." He smirked at her stunned expression. "You didn't think that suddenly you were the lady of the house, did you?" He brushed by her and walked out.

Marcia saw her entire future walking out the door. She'd watched Dominique's slow downward spiral over the past few months, the way she started drinking more and more and how Clifton was out of the house more than he was in. Marcia always made sure that there was a bottle close by to keep Dominique company. If Dominique couldn't hold on to her man, could she blame Marcia for stepping in to fill her shoes?

She looked around, turning in a slow circle. Five years she'd worked toward having Clifton Burrell as her own. She'd stayed in the background, listening, waiting. She knew Clifton ran around with other women, she'd intercepted some of the calls, overheard his whispered conversations. That didn't matter to her, she knew they were simply distractions. She understood how difficult it must have been for him to often be referred to as *Mr. Laws,* husband to the star. So she made sure she made Clifton feel important and valuable every chance she got. Whatever he wanted, he rarely had to ask. It was done. She anticipated his needs. And he showed his appreciation with that sexy smile or a little something extra in her pay, small secret gifts. "This is for you," he'd say, coming up behind her in the kitchen or in the washroom. "Just to say thanks."

"I really appreciate all the little things you do for me," she'd said to him a month earlier when they were alone out on the patio. "I know you don't have to." Her gaze locked on to his.

A slow, easy smile moved across his mouth. He leaned against the pillar supporting the deck and folded his arms. "You appreciate it, huh?" He ran his tongue slowly across his lips. "How much?"

Her heart thudded. "Very much," she said with a slight lift of her chin.

Clifton took one step, then another, until he was right in front of her, forcing her to look up at him. "Is that right?" His dark eyes grazed over her face, heating her from the inside out. She wondered if he could hear the pounding of her heart. "We'll have to see about that."

She knew what they were doing was wrong, but she couldn't help herself. She'd lusted after Clifton Burrell from the moment she'd been hired five years earlier. Now was her time. She could make him happy. She could make him stop running from woman to woman. She could make him leave Dominique and love her the way she loved him. She knew it with every fiber of her being. And she tried to prove it to him right there under the beat of the morning sun, up against the wall of the deck. With every thrust, every moan, she vowed not to make this the last time.

It hadn't been.

Every chance they got they were together. Clifton was insatiable, taking her wherever and whenever the opportunity presented itself. She never denied him. Never.

Now it was over. He thought he could simply pay her off like a high-priced hooker and tell her to be on her way? She sucked in air through her nostrils as she swiped at the steady steam of tears with the back of her hand. She marched into the hall and spotted the white envelope on the table. She grabbed it up and opened it. There was a cashier's check for five thousand dollars inside, with Severance Pay written on the note line. She folded the check and put it in her pocket, then stared at the front door. She may walk out of it but she would be far from gone. Clifton Burrell could bet on that.

It wasn't often that Clifton had attacks of conscience. It was such a rare occurrence it could only be categorized with the likes of a solar eclipse. But his conscience nagged at him. The weight of guilt sat on the center of his chest like an anvil. He knew he was partly to blame for what was going on with Dominique. He'd watched silently, sometimes accusingly, as she had begun to unravel. She was always fragile, sometimes too fragile, the slightest thing rocking her. What did he expect would happen when all he did was run around with other women, talk down to her whenever the mood hit him? Sometimes he didn't know why he did any of it. Other times his reasons were clear as French-cut crystal—he felt emasculated. As Dominique's star rose, his sense of worth declined. It was as simple as that. So he found ways to boost his manhood with women, with making Dominique feel small and ineffectual. It gave him some measure of satisfaction at least for a little while. This time, however, he'd gotten in too deep, taken things too far. He had to find a way to make amends or everything would surely come apart.

Manny's house was up ahead. He put on his signal and turned onto his street. For several moments he sat in the car rehearsing his lines. He could act, too, when the need arose.

He walked up to the front door and rang the bell. Several moments later, the housekeeper answered the door.

"Mr. Burrell, was Mr. Breevort expecting you?"

"No. He wasn't. Is he in?"

"I'm sorry, he isn't. But Mrs. Breevort is home. Should I get her for you?"

"Yes."

"Come in."

Clifton followed the housekeeper inside and

waited in the sitting room. Shortly, Evelyn walked in, her patrician features stretched taut and her blue eyes looked dark and angry like the ocean before a storm.

"What can I do for you, Clif?" She stood in the doorway.

"I want to know where Dominique is."

"She's not here."

"I saw the paper." He looked sheepish. "I haven't heard from her. I was sure she'd contact Manny."

Evelyn's thin lips tightened. "Dominique is far from fine but she will be, if that's what you want to know."

"You have seen her."

She didn't reply. Manny told her not to say a word to anyone about where Dominique was, especially not to Clif.

He took a menacing step toward her. "Where is she, Evelyn?"

"I have no idea."

"You're a liar."

"And you're a bastard. Now get out of my house."

"Where is she? She's my wife. You can't keep her from me."

Evelyn was not impressed. "Get out," she said in a cool monotone.

Clifton's chest puffed in and out. He looked like he would explode. The pulse in his temple visibly pounded.

Without another word he turned around and stormed to his car.

Evelyn's body slumped. For a moment she had thought he might actually strike her. She'd never seen that look in Clifton's eyes before. It was chilling. Wherever Manny had taken Dominique, she hoped it was far away and out of Clifton Burrell's reach.

When Clifton drew close to his home, he saw several vans parked outside on the street. *The media has descended.* He knew it was only a matter of time. He drove past them and up to the gate that guarded his property.

The instant his car was spotted, reporters jumped out of the vans and joined the photographers that lined the street. They mobbed his car, flashing their cameras in his face and shouting for a statement.

"Where is your wife?"

"Is it true that she tried to commit suicide?

"What are your comments about the pictures in *Star?*"

"Give us a statement!"

He used the remote in his car to open the gate. It seemed to open in slow motion. When there was enough room for him to drive through, he darted in and set the remote to close the gates behind him. The one saving grace was that he knew they wouldn't dare come across the gate for fear of being prosecuted for trespassing.

That didn't keep them from calling. The phone was ringing from the moment he walked in the door and didn't stop all day. It baffled him how they were always able to secure unlisted numbers.

He had to figure something out. He had to find Dominique. He knew things were going to get worse before they got better, of that he was certain.

And they did.

# Chapter 10

"I don't want to stay here," Dominique was saying.

"It's for your own good, Dominique. You're not well."

"I'm fine. I just need a drink and I'll be fine."

Sweat seeped through every pore. Her body trembled.

"Please. Just one little one," she said holding up a shaky finger.

"You can get through this."

"I don't want to get through it!" She jerked up in the bed, rattling the metal railings. Her eyes were wild and glazed.

The nurse rushed in. "Please step outside, Mr. Breevort."

Manny took a look at Dominique's tortured expression and slowly turned and walked out.

During the night Dominique had grown violently ill, her body in pain, her mind on a rampage. Manny and Evelyn grew frightened for her, sure that she would do something to hurt herself. Manny called his private doctor, who came to the house and administered a sedative.

"She's experiencing withdrawal and what I think is alcohol poisoning. She needs to be in a hospital where she can be looked after and monitored," the doctor had said, leaving the guest room once he'd quieted her down.

"It will be a media fest if I take her into a hospital." Manny ran his hand across his face.

"I can make some calls and get her in discretely under an assumed name."

"Will you do that?"

"Of course. Where's your phone?"

Manny took him to the phone and waited while the doctor spoke in hushed tones.

"Okay." He blew out a long breath. "She's sedated. She probably won't wake up until morning. We can take her in my car to St. Vincent's Medical Center. It's small and private. I have privileges there."

"Thank you." He offered a tight smile. "I'll have Evelyn help me get her ready."

So here Dominique was, or rather Cynthia Bowen. The doctors said it would take a least a few days to get her stabilized, she would need to go into rehab as soon as she left the hospital.

His next hurdle was convincing Dominique that she must enter rehab if she ever wanted to be well.

The nurse came out and quietly closed the door. "I gave her another mild sedative. She's not asleep but she's calm."

Manny nodded. "Thank you. Can I go back in?"

"Yes."

Manny pushed open the door and stepped inside. She looked so tiny and fragile beneath the white sheets. An IV drip was in her arm that was tied to the bed. Manny's heart broke. How could things have gotten this bad? He pulled up a chair next to the bed and sat down. He took her hand and rubbed it gently. "It's going to be okay, Dom."

Slowly she turned her head in his direction. A semblance of a smile drifted to her mouth. "Promise?"

"Promise."

She closed her eyes and drifted off to sleep. Manny reached for the remote and turned on the television.

"Oh, my God," he whispered.

"Alan! Alan, come and look at this," Adrienne called out from the living room of their modest home in the suburbs of Atlanta.

Alan walked into the room with a cup of coffee in his hand. "What is it?"

She pointed to the television screen. There was a close-up of someone who appeared to be Dominique Laws. Alan frowned and drew closer to listen to the broadcast.

"Those are images taken yesterday morning at a motel in South Central Los Angeles of Golden Globe nominee Dominique Laws. According to reporters on the scene, Ms. Laws was disheveled and obviously inebriated."

The next clip was an interview with a motel clerk.

"The lady come in two weeks ago, pay me in cash and never come out of her room except for more something to drink. I think it strange, but—" he shrugged his shoulders "—she pay me."

"Did you know who she was when she came in?"

"*Sí, sí.*" He bobbed his head.

"It was you who called the reporters, is that correct?"

"*Sí.* I thought she was maybe here to make a movie." He grinned showing his brown teeth. "And it would make my place famous, you know."

The scene cut back to the studio. "According to Ms. Laws's agent, Manny Breevort, who came to take Ms. Laws out of the motel, she was there to rehearse. However, the story continues to take on a new twist. Here is an interview done just moments ago with Marcia Kensington, the longtime housekeeper for Ms. Laws and her husband and manager, Clifton Burrell.

"Ms. Laws hasn't been herself for a while." Marcia momentarily lowered her head, then looked at the reporter with innocent doe-eyes. "So Mr. Laws turned to me. We tried to find a way to tell her, but she found out on her own. And now with the baby on the way…"

"Are you saying you're pregnant by Ms. Laws's husband?"

"Yes."

Adrienne spun toward her husband, hands on hips with a look of triumph on her face. "Those rich folks are something else. She's a drunk and her husband is a sleaze. And there they were trying to act all uppity. Hmph." She breezed out of the room. "Looks sure can be deceiving," she tossed over her shoulder.

Alan slowly sat down on the couch and flipped through the channels, every station had one version or another about the story.

Looks *can* be deceiving, Alan concurred, but eyes didn't lie. As a filmmaker that's what he looked for, the soul of a person through their eyes. It took more than speaking the words and projecting the perfect facial expressions to make a person or a character come alive. When the camera moved in on the face, the eyes told the truth.

He'd seen the truth in Dominique's eyes. The loneliness and the unhappiness, all shielded behind a facade of picture-perfection. He could only imagine what must have driven her to the depths to which she'd sunken. Had she known about the affair between her husband and her housekeeper? And now, if there was any truth to the housekeeper's story, there was a baby on the way.

Sadly he shook his head. He had the overwhelming desire to talk to her or rather to take her in his arms and hold her close. Dominique Laws had touched him in a way that he had been sure was dead and buried. He'd resigned himself to the fact that he would be forever tied to Adrienne, through guilt and obligation. But when he met Dominique that night at the Globes, for the first time in years he felt the inklings of hope, the kernel of belief that there was life beyond the sham he was living. He felt his feelings stir, feelings that had been dormant too long. From that day right up until this moment, his thoughts had been filled with her. He may not be cheating on his wife the way Clifton had physically cheated on his, but he was cheating on Adrienne in his mind.

When they made love he envisioned Dominique beneath him. It was her lush lips that he kissed, her body that he satisfied. When he would open his eyes and look upon Adrienne, a wave of disappointment would fill him. It was all a fantasy. Adrienne and the empty life he lived with her was his reality.

He got up and walked to the window. She would surely divorce Clifton after this. Then she would be free. But what then?

The phone rang, jarring him away from his wandering thoughts. He crossed the room and picked it up.

"Yes?"

"Hey man, it's Brian."

"Hey, what's going on?"

"Do I have good news or what?" he said, the excitement in his voice barely contained.

"Spill it, spill it."

"We got the financing. We got it!"

"What!" Alan slapped his palm against his forehead. "You're not just pulling my chain, are you?"

"Not about something like this. They want to meet with us tomorrow morning in New York to sign the deal."

"Tomorrow?"

"Don't sweat it, they'll have the tickets waiting for us at the counter."

"Oh, man," he said in awe. "I believe it, but I don't believe it." He laughed. "It's been a long time coming. You worked it, brother."

"You know I did. Now we'll have our own studio, be able to make the kinds of movies we want to make."

Alan spun in a circle. This was their dream, what they'd worked years to accomplish. Sure he'd had his share of success with independent and studio films. He'd even won awards. But this was big. Now he could call the shots, or rather, he and Brian could call the shots.

"What time is the flight?"

"Pack your bag. We're outta here tonight. Seven o'clock outta Hatfield."

Alan checked his watch. It was already past two. He needed to get it together. With all the security at the airports, you could never get there too early.

"Oh, did I mention we were flying first class?" Brian chuckled.

"The best for the best. Let me get a move on and tell Adrienne." He dreaded that part, sure that she would throw some kind of tantrum.

"See you at the airport. Oh, we're flying American Airlines."

"Cool. See you there." He hung up. Elation nearly lifted him off the ground. He balled his fist and fired it through the air. This was it. Finally.

He jogged upstairs to find Adrienne.

"You're leaving? Today?"

"Yeah, babe." He clasped her arms and stared into her eyes. "This is it, what we've been waiting for— our own studio with a budget."

"But why today? Don't they know you have a life? You can't just pick up and go at the drop of a hat. I don't care who they are."

Alan drew in a short breath. "Baby, when things like this happen you jump on it. Money people don't sit around and wait for you to get ready to take their money. I'll be back day after tomorrow."

She huffed. "I want to go with you."

"Baby the tickets are already paid for. You can't go. Besides I wouldn't have any time to spend with you. It's a business meeting, that's it."

She pulled away from him. "You're going to see *her* aren't you? That's the truth. Why don't you just tell me the truth?"

"A, I'm not going to see anyone. I'm going with Brian, your brother."

"I saw the way you looked at her, Alan." Her voice turned to a soft whine. "She's not prettier than me. You saw her on television. She's ugly." Suddenly she grabbed him. "I don't want to lose you, Alan. I love you." Her hands clasped both sides of his face. She pressed her voluptuous body fully against his, rotating her pelvis against him. "I can make you happy. Don't I always make you happy, Alan?"

"Yes, A, you always make me happy."

She reached down and massaged him the way she knew he liked it, smiling as his erection sprouted in her hand.

"A, please, baby, not now."

"Yes, now," she said against his mouth. "I'm your wife. Make me happy." She caressed him even more until he felt as if he would explode.

Need for release overrode rationale. He took her in his arms and to bed.

While Adrienne dozed, Alan prepared for his trip. He moved soundlessly around the room so as not to disturb her. The last thing he needed was eleventh-hour histrionics, which Adrienne was famous for. He left a note on the dresser with promises to call her as soon as the plane landed and then eased out of the room.

* * *

While Alan and Brian waited in the holding area for their flight, the overhead televisions were broadcasting the news. A repeat of the earlier broadcast about Dominique came on the screen.

"Did you see this, man?" Brian asked, finishing off a sandwich.

"Yeah, saw it earlier."

"Damn shame. I was thinking of her for some of our upcoming projects, especially after hubby invited you to the house. I know it was to schmooze you. If she ever gets out from under all of this it'll be a miracle."

Alan stared at the disturbing images. Yeah, it would be a miracle.

The announcement came over the intercom that first-class passengers could begin boarding.

"That's us," Brian said, grinning.

Alan winked, picked up his carry-on and headed for the gate behind Brian, just as he felt the vibration of his cell phone go off. He pulled the cell phone from the case and checked the number. It was Adrienne. He hesitated, debating about whether or not to answer. He decided against it. He was sure it was only to harass him about the trip followed by a series of whining and pleading. He shut off his cell phone. When he landed he would call as he'd promised. She'd just have to hold it together until then.

## Chapter 11

"They want to release you in a couple of days, Dominique," Manny was saying to her the following morning. According to the hospital staff, she'd spent a quiet night and had not been sedated. She'd even had something to eat that morning. He'd had the television removed from her room while she'd slept, hoping to keep that last bit of ugly news away from her for as long as possible.

"I can't go home," she murmured. "I won't go back there with him." She shook her head and squeezed her eyes shut.

"I know and I understand." He pulled his chair closer to the bed. "You need help, Dominique.

There's only so much the doctors here can do for you."

"What are you saying?" She opened her eyes and looked at him.

"You need to get into rehab. You have a problem."

She turned away. "I don't have a problem. I have a screwed-up life and a bastard for a husband. Can rehab fix that?"

"They can help you fix it."

"Yeah, right. So you're saying I'm crazy or something?"

"No, that's not what I'm saying. But you've been depressed, under a lot of pressure and you've been drinking too much. You're on a course of destruction and I'm not going to sit back and let that happen. You could have killed yourself."

"I wish I was dead."

"No, you don't. You wish your life were different."

"I'm not going to rehab."

"You need to, even the doctors said so."

"I'm not going. They can't fix what's broken."

"And you can't do it by yourself."

She turned to him, the old fire and defiance back in her eyes. "Yes, I can and I will. You can either support me or not. It's your choice."

He stared at her for a long moment, knowing that arguing with her was futile. The doctors had warned him that she might balk at the idea of going into recovery and that the only way it would work was if she was willing and mentally ready. It was apparent that she was neither.

"Fine. So what are you going to do?"

"I'm going to get out of this hospital, find a hotel—a good one," she emphasized, "and get a divorce lawyer." She looked him in the eyes. "That's what I'm going to do."

Manny smirked. "Fine. Do you need my help?"

"You can recommend a good hotel and a damned good attorney."

"I'll get right on it." He folded his hands on his lap and took a short breath. "Dom, there's something else. I want to be the one to tell you before you hear it on the news or read it in the papers."

"What could be worse than what's already happened?"

"Allegedly, Marcia is pregnant by Clifton."

Her expression froze for a second. Her nostrils flared. "I see."

"They interviewed her on the news." She glanced up, noticed for the first time that there was no television and quickly concluded that it was Manny's doing.

The sick sensation was back in her stomach again. What a fool she'd been made of. Not only was her husband screwing around, but now he'd gotten his mistress pregnant! How many years had she told Clifton that she wanted a child, a child of their own? And every time he'd say, *not now, think of your career, there's always time for kids.* Another little piece of her died inside.

"I hope they're very happy together." She drew in air. "I'd really like you to find me a lawyer as soon as possible."

"Of course, and I'll check into some hotels."

"Nothing in Beverly Hills, nothing in L.A., period, maybe something near San Francisco, around Vallejo."

Manny nodded. "I'll take care of that for you today. If I can't find anything, you know you're welcome to come and stay with me and Evelyn."

She shook her head. "No. I need to be on my own. And I don't want to impose on you and your wife. You've done enough for me already, way above and beyond the call of agent duty." She tried to laugh. It sounded strained.

He took her hand in his. "You're more than a client, Dominique, you're a friend. I want you to know that."

"I appreciate that. Looks like I'm going to need all the friends I can get."

"Ready, buddy?" Brian asked as he adjusted his tie.

"As I'll ever be." Alan put on his jacket and stuck his cell phone in its case. He still had not heard back from Adrienne, which was odd. Maybe she was just pissed off that he'd left and was having one of her silent tantrums. He'd called when he'd landed, as promised, and called again before bed and again when he got up. Each time his calls went to voice mail. He'd try her again when he returned from the meeting.

"Everything okay?" Brian asked. "You look… tense."

Alan laughed it off. "This is a tense moment." He chucked Brian in the upper arm. "I'm good. Just putting on my game face."

"All righty, let's do this."

Brian and Alan were met in the hotel lobby by the driver sent to take them to their meeting.

"The car is out front, gentleman," the driver said, leading them outside.

Brian leaned over to Alan. "Now this is what I call the star treatment," Brian whispered.

"The best for the best," Alan replied.

The got into the limo and zipped in and out of the midtown Manhattan traffic.

"It's hard to believe this place is really an island," Brian said.

"I know. It's an incredible city. Never a dull moment. I wish they had more production studios out here."

"DeNiro has a spot down in Tribeca. The big problem with filming in New York is the cost. But now that we have financing, it's certainly an option."

"I'd really love to shoot something here. There're definitely enough locations to choose from. You have all the paperwork, right?"

Brian tapped his leather briefcase. "Got it."

Alan nodded and sat back in the plush leather

seat, taking in the bustling scenery as they drove. But then his mind shifted to Adrienne. As much as he didn't want to, he was beginning to worry. It wasn't like her not to call at least after a few attempts at trying to reach her. She would call back if only to get under his skin. There wasn't much he could do about it now. He'd give her another call after the meeting.

They arrived at the corporate offices of Stevens and Howard Enterprises on Madison Avenue. As expected, the twentieth-floor offices were state-of-the-art glass and chrome, with thick carpets and soundproof rooms. They were escorted to an enclosed lounge.

"Can I get you gentlemen anything?" the receptionist asked.

"Nothing for me," Alan said.

"Some water would be great," Brian answered.

"Be right back."

Alan looked around. "This place reeks of money," he said jokingly.

"And I love the smell."

They chuckled.

The receptionist returned with a tray holding a bottle of water and a crystal glass and cloth napkin. She set them down on a glass table. "Mr. Howard and Mr. Stevens will be with you shortly. I'll come and get you when they're ready."

"Thank you," they said in unison.

"Nervous?" Alan asked.

Brian shrugged. "A little. I don't want to get in there and forget my name." He chuckled. "I think it'll go fine. They simply want to meet us face-to-face and go over some of the fine points."

Alan nodded.

The receptionist returned. "They're ready for you. If you'll follow me, I'll take you up."

They rode the elevator to the thirtieth floor. The doors opened to an area even more lush than the one they'd left. Instead of glass and chrome, the fixtures were all imported hardwood, gold-plated names hung on the doors. They proceeded down the corridor to another receptionist.

"This is Mr. Conners and Mr. Chambers."

"I'll take them right in."

The first receptionist smiled at them and left.

"If you'll follow me, your meeting is in the main conference room."

They went down another hallway until they reached the conference room. The young woman opened the door for them.

A dozen sets of eyes turned in their direction.

"Now I'm nervous," Brian whispered, walking in behind Alan.

"Gentlemen." He came to the door to greet them. "Kevin Stevens."

Alan and Brian introduced themselves.

"Join us. We're anxious to talk to you. These are the members of our team." Kevin introduced everyone. "Unfortunately, Mr. Howard couldn't be here today. He had a last-minute appointment that couldn't be changed."

He showed them to their seats and the meeting began. What Stevens and Howard were willing to do was to finance all the start-up costs associated with launching their production company as well as providing the financing for their first five projects, up to a cap of three million each.

"We've gone over all of your figures and your proposal for your upcoming projects. Everything looks good. Your presentation, Mr. Chambers, was flawless and we've all reviewed the wonderful work you've done, Mr. Conners. However, we want to do a few more adjustments to our offer and that won't be done until Mr. Howard returns tonight. So, I'm hoping that you will enjoy our hospitality, stay another night and meet back with us tomorrow."

Alan and Brian looked at each other, not expecting that last bit of information.

"Of course," Brian finally said.

"Great." Kevin stood. "So tomorrow at noon. We can have you on a plane back to Atlanta by six. How's that?"

"Fine," Alan said.

Kevin came around the massive table to walk them to the door. "My secretary will escort you downstairs. Great meeting both of you." He shook their hands before they walked out.

Back in the limo Alan and Brian were contemplative.

"You don't think they're going to pull out, do you?" Brian asked, finally breaking the silence.

"I don't think pull out, but maybe not finance as much as they originally offered. I guess Howard must hold the purse strings."

"Hmm." He blew out a long breath. "We gotta make this happen. We're so close." He tightened his fist.

Alan knew how hard and how many months Brian had worked on wearing folks down and getting behind previously closed doors to make this meeting happen. He knew *he* would take it hard if it somehow fell through, but Brian would be devastated. "It'll be all right, buddy," he said, patting Brian's thigh.

"Yeah," he said in a faraway voice.

When they got back to the hotel, the first thing Alan did was try to reach Adrienne again. Still nothing but voice mail. Now he was worried. Something was definitely wrong.

# Chapter 12

Still no word from Dominique. Clifton contemplated his next move. The first thing on his agenda was to deal with Marcia. There was no way she was going to strap him with a child. He should have never gotten involved with her in the first place, but she pretty much threw herself at him and swore that there were no strings attached.

At first she was a pleasant diversion and another way for him to assert himself as Clifton Burrell, not the husband of the star.

It was like that with all the women he'd bedded during his marriage to Dominique. There was no love—sometimes not even lust—simply a way to convince himself that he could do something beyond being Dominique's husband.

Over the years his role and Dominique's had changed. In the beginning, he was in control; he called the shots and made all the decisions. But as her popularity grew and the demand for her increased, his importance diminished. In turn, he became vindictive and hostile toward her, looking for ways to bring her down. When he was able to chip away at her emotions, he felt stronger. But it never lasted, so the cycle would begin again. He deserved the accolades, the spotlight in the news. He was the one responsible for the Dominique Laws that the world had come to know. Without him, she was nothing. Nothing.

He snatched up his jacket and headed for the front door. This thing with Marcia had ruined everything. She'd forced his hand. He'd thought when Dominique caught him in the act, it would compel her to beg him to stay with her. She would profess her love for him, her need for him. But it hadn't worked that way.

Clifton got in his car, pleased that the reporters apparently had found some other hot story to exploit and had left the front of his property. He sped away. This thing with Marcia was going to be settled today and then he would finish what he'd started. If he was to live a life without Dominique, he wasn't going to live it empty-handed.

He parked across the street from Marcia's apartment complex and walked to the front of her building, the first in a cluster of six. He found her bell and rang.

Several moments passed before he heard the crackling of the intercom and Marcia's voice.

"It's Clif. We need to talk." He waited. Finally the door buzzed and he pushed his way in. He walked down the short hall to her apartment. The door opened before he reached it. Marcia stood in the doorway.

"What is it?"

"What do you think you're doing, lying to the media? Are you crazy?"

"No. I'm pregnant with your child!"

He walked right up on her. "Look, if you think for one minute that you're going to railroad me, you have another thing coming. It's not happening."

"You can't just toss me aside. Use me when you want and walk away. I won't have it. Maybe you can walk all over your wife, but not me." She stared right into his eyes and didn't flinch.

"I'm warning you, Marcia, don't screw with me. You'll regret it."

"Are you threatening me?"

"Take it any way you want, but you're not getting a dime from me. Ever! I'll make sure of that. I'll drag you through every court and tabloid in the country if I have to. By the time I'm finished with you, you won't even own your name." He glared at her for a moment then spun around and stormed out of the building. He heard her apartment door slam as he was leaving.

Clifton got behind the wheel of his car. He was breathing deeply. Hopefully he'd shaken Marcia up enough to keep her out of his hair until he could tie up some loose ends. It had been two weeks since he'd seen or heard from Dominique. He was pretty sure she had no intentions of coming back, and if and when she did he would be gone.

"Don't you want to go by the house and pick up some of your things?" Manny asked Dominique as the nurse wheeled her to the hospital exit.

Images of Clifton and Marcia flashed through her head and her resolve stiffened. "No. I'm not going back there. The house is in my name, bought with my hard-earned money. I want to put it on the market immediately."

"As long as you're sure. I can go with you."

"No, Manny. I don't want to talk about it anymore."

They got out front and Dominique stood. The nurse took the chair and left them.

"The car is over there." Manny helped her to the car and got her settled inside. "I thought you might be a bit more comfortable in something small and private instead of in a hotel. I took the liberty of renting you a small cottage in Vallejo. It's fully furnished, near all of the necessities."

"I'm sure it will be fine." She put on her dark glasses and leaned back. This was more than a drive away from a short hospital stay, she was en route to a new life. Nothing would ever be the same again. She had some thinking to do, some decisions to make on how she was going to move on from here. For so long there was always someone, somewhere, who made all the decisions for her: Clif, Manny, a director, a photographer, a stylist. She never had to think about anything other than her lines and how she was going to make a character come to life. Her decision-making skills were rusty and she was scared, but she knew she could do it. She had no choice.

"Were you able to find an attorney?"

"I've talked with several, discretely of course. I'll go over them with you when we get you…home."

She turned to him. "I know I haven't said it, but thank you for everything. I don't know what I would have done if you hadn't been there."

"I told you I'm more than just your agent, Dom, I'm your friend. You're going to be fine." He paused. "Uh, I've been speaking with your publicist and we've been working on a damage-control plan. The story has died down a bit with all the new celebrity scandals that brew from one day to the next. But the moment you resurface it will all come crashing back. However, we feel that we can use all the negative publicity to our advantage."

"Advantage?" She chuckled. "You mean make lemonade out of lemons."

"Something like that." He glanced at her then turned back to the road. "In about a week or two, we wanted to set up some interviews with you for a couple of mags and do some TV spots. Use the whole betrayal issue to your advantage. You were the one victimized by this whole thing."

She shook her head. "No."

"Why not?"

"I don't know what I want to do right now, especially about my career. It was going downhill before… all of this."

"And when one door closes another opens. Maybe all this ugliness was a blessing in disguise."

"You've got to be kidding."

"No, I'm not. If you simply sit back then you will be a victim. And you're better than that. I know it and you know it."

She sighed heavily and stared out the passenger window. "I'll think about it, but I'm not promising anything."

"Good enough."

As they headed toward her new abode Dominique came up short in the car. "Wait." She clasped Manny's arm. "There is something I need to get from the house."

"Not a problem." He made the next turn and headed back toward Beverly Hills.

Dominique chewed on her thumbnail. What if Clifton was there? What if Marcia was there or reporters? She started to perspire. Her heart beat faster. She could do it. She'd simply breeze right by them as if they didn't exist. She gripped the armrest for the rest of the ride.

When the pulled onto her street she released a silent breath of relief. There were no TV vans in sight and she didn't see Clifton's car.

"I'll be right out," Dominique said, jumping out of the car and looking around as if she were a thief in fear of being caught.

Her heart was racing so fast she could barely breathe. She jogged up to the front door, took out her key and opened the door. The telltale beep of the alarm greeted her. She quickly disengaged the alarm. The last thing she needed was the police descending on her.

She took a quick look around then darted up to her bedroom. When she flung open the door she felt as if she had been hit with a powerful gust of wind. She wobbled in the doorway. The bed she'd shared with Clifton seemed to mock her. For a moment she squeezed her eyes shut to ward off the images of him in bed with Marcia. She tugged in a long breath and went to her closet. On the top shelf she pulled down her journal. It was the only thing she wanted. She took one last look around and left.

Just as she got to the bottom of the stairs, the front door opened. Clifton stood in the doorway with Manny directly behind him.

Dominique descended the stairs regally.

She tried to walk past Clifton. He grabbed her arm.

"Why haven't you answered my calls? Where have you been?"

"Take your hand off me, Clif," she said, her voice chillingly calm.

Manny stepped up. "Clif…"

"Stay out of this, Manny. This is between me and my wife."

"Your wife! How dare you?" Dominique railed. "You don't do to your wife what you did to me. Get out of my way, Clif." Her steely gaze bore into him.

Clif was visibly taken aback by Dominique's vehemence. In all the years he'd known her she'd never challenged him.

"The only conversation we'll have is through our attorneys." She pushed past him leaving Clif in open-mouthed silence.

"Are you okay?" Manny asked as he helped her into the car.

"Fine." She was shaking all over but in a good way. She felt a sense of relief, a weight lifted from her soul. "Fine," she repeated.


"You've been distracted for the past couple of days," Brian said as they prepared for their noon meeting. "What gives?"

Alan frowned. "I've been trying to reach Adrienne since we arrived and I haven't gotten an answer. I left countless messages and she hasn't returned any of my calls. It's not like her."

"Let me call Stacy and have her go over there. Knowing Adrienne, she's probably either shopping or pouting," he said, trying to sound lighthearted.

"Yeah, but give Stacy a call anyway."

"Sure." He pulled out his cell phone and dialed his wife. The voice mail came on. "Hey babe, listen, when you get this message, I need you to go check on Adrienne. Alan's been trying to reach her and he hasn't been able to. Give me a call back when you talk to her. Love you." He disconnected the call. "She's probably out somewhere." He looked at Alan. "I'm sure she's fine." He patted Alan's back. "Come on, let's nail this deal down and go home to our lovely wives."

Alan forced a smile and followed Brian.

The meeting went better than planned. When they left they were ecstatic and carrying a big fat check.

"Damn, man I feel like we need those brothers from Brink's security to roll with us," Brian joked, looking at the cashier's check for two million dollars, the first deposit on their dream.

"Wow," Alan breathed, "I still can't believe it. Not only will they pay for the first few projects, but they upped the money."

"The type of work we want to do will redefine black film. Howard and Stevens are visionaries and risk takers. There's a reason why they are only one of two major black finance companies listed with Fortune 500. Those guys are major players."

Alan's eyes sparkled. "I can finally do the kinds of films I want," he said with awe. Immediately he thought of Dominique and all that she'd been through. A picture deal with him might put her back on top where she belonged. He imagined working with her every day, seeing her every day and what that would be like. Then he wondered if he would be able to temper his attraction to her during the process. He would have to; she was a married woman and, for all intents and purposes, he was a married man.

Brian's cell phone rang halfway back to the hotel. The moment he answered, Alan could hear the high pitch of Stacy's voice. Brian's face literally paled. His mouth opened and closed but no words came out.

Alan grabbed his jacket sleeve. "B, what is it?"

He was nodding his head as if Stacy could see him. "We'll be on the next flight." He shut off the phone and turned tortured eyes on Alan. "It's Adrienne…"

## Chapter 13

Manny pulled up in front of Dominique's rented house. It was on a quiet cul de sac along with only three other houses. Hers was at the end. He helped her out of the car and into the house.

Dominique looked around at the simple furnishings and the comforting space. It was certainly smaller than anything she'd lived in over the past decade, but in truth this was all she needed.

Manny gave her the short tour of the one-bedroom setup. "So…what do you think?"

She bobbed her head. "Very nice. I like it." She turned to him with a soft smile. "Thank you."

"Not a problem. The house is rented for three

months. I thought that would be enough time for you to decide what you wanted to do."

She drew in a breath.

"I also took the liberty of having Evelyn pick out some things for you so that you would be comfortable, dishes and pots, linens, things like that. The fridge is also full."

Her eyes filled and she sniffed back tears. "How did it all come to this?" she said, her voice breaking.

Manny came to her and pulled her close. "It's going to be okay. I promise you."

She wiped away her tears. "I can't keep falling apart at the drop of a hat, that's for sure." She sniffed.

"You're entitled. For a little while," he qualified, which drew a weak smile from her. "You want me to hang around for a bit or would you rather be alone?"

"You've done enough. I'll be fine. You must have other needy clients hanging around somewhere." She wiped her eyes.

Manny chuckled. "That I do. Well, I'll give you a call tomorrow and set up those appointments with the attorneys."

"Good. The sooner the better." She walked him to the door.

Manny leaned down and kissed her cheek. "Get some rest. We'll talk tomorrow."

She closed the door and through the window she watched him drive away. She turned and took in her space. It wasn't so bad. Her stomach suddenly grumbled. She was actually hungry. That was a good sign and she headed for the kitchen to see what Evelyn had purchased.

Just as Manny said, the fridge was stocked. Evelyn was a health-food nut and it showed in her selections. Whole wheat this, low-carb and no-fat that, bottles of imported water and fresh juices.

She opted for a sandwich of honey turkey, with Dijon mustard on a pita roll and something that looked like shredded grass for a little color and extra flavor. She took out a bottle of mango juice and went into the cozy living room.

Seated on the small off-white sofa, she located the remote and turned on the television. The local talk show cut away for breaking news. She held her breath praying that it had nothing to do with her.

The scene was one of the usual chaos, with ambulances, reporters and police cars in the background. The images were being broadcast from Atlanta. She sat up and turned up the volume.

"Earlier this morning, the body of Adrienne Conners, wife of filmmaker and director Alan Conners, was found by her bother's wife, Stacy Chambers."

Dominique's heart began to thud as she listened.

"According to the medical examiner on the scene, it is an apparent overdose. But there will be no final determination until an autopsy is performed."

There was a flurry of activity in the background.

The reporter turned. Dominique's pulse thundered when she spotted him.

"Alan Conners, husband of the deceased has just arrived. He's being escorted into the home by police officers on the scene." The reporter pressed her finger to her earpiece then looked in the camera. "According to information just received, Mr. Conners was out of town on a business trip when he received the call. This is Robin Masterson for KLS News. Back to the studio."

"Tragic," the in-studio anchor murmured with just the right amount of sorrow etched on his face. "Now in other news…"

Dominique turned off the television. For a while she sat there stunned, her food untouched. She couldn't imagine what Alan must be going through. To come home and find… She had an overwhelming desire to contact him, to at least share her condolences. It was so odd the connection she felt with him, as if they'd always known each other. Her heart ached—knowing the media as she did, it was only a matter of time before every piece of his laundry was tossed out on the lawn for inspection.

Suddenly she jumped up and hurried into the bedroom. She picked up her purse and rifled through it, finally locating what she was looking for. He'd left his business card at the house the night of the dinner party. She stared at the number. Of course, now wasn't the time to call, maybe tomorrow.

She drew in a breath of resolve. Yes, tomorrow she

would call him and tell him how sorry she was. That would be it, just that she was sorry for his loss, nothing more. She looked at the number again before pressing it to her chest. *It'll be okay. Promise.*

Alan and Brian sat in his living room limp with grief and disbelief even as the police and the medical examiner's team worked around them.

"When was the last time you spoke to your wife?" a detective was asking Alan.

He raised his head to look at the detective. "Right before I left for New York." His voice was distant. He swallowed. "She was asleep."

The detective perked up. "Asleep? Are you sure? Had she taken something?"

Alan shook his head. "No. She… We had just made love and…she'd fallen asleep. I didn't want to wake her…. Oh, God." He covered his face.

Brian patted him on the back. "Can we do this later, detective?"

"I know it's difficult but it's always best to get as much information as possible as soon as possible. The more time passes…people tend to forget.

"Has your wife had any problems recently, something that would push her to do something like this?"

Alan's expression pinched in pain. "Adrienne was always a little high-strung. She didn't want me to go to New York, but that was nothing out of the ordinary."

"Did you know that your wife had a supply of

Valium and sleeping pills, Mr. Conners?" He stared hard at Alan.

"No, I didn't."

"Hmm. And you say she was asleep when you left?"

"Yes," Alan barked out.

"Had she ever taken anything before to help her sleep?"

"No, not that I know of. I told you I had no idea she had that stuff."

The detective made some notes then flipped his pad shut. He stood. "I'm very sorry for your loss, Mr. Conners, Mr. Chambers. I'm sure after the medical examiner determines cause of death I'll be back in touch with you."

Alan followed him with his eyes as he went to talk with another group of police.

"Why would she do something like this?" Brian said to no one in particular. "She seemed happy."

"Maybe it was just a horrible accident. I don't know…"

Stacy approached, her eyes red rimmed. She sat down beside her husband. "I'm so sorry, Alan."

He nodded his head. "I wish you weren't the one who had to find her." He glanced away and myriad dark thoughts raced through his head. Did she do this intentionally? Was she that sick? His conscience tugged at him. He'd known for a while that Adrienne was becoming more and more…unstable, but often he simply attributed it to her neediness. But deep down he knew it was more than that. He'd wanted her to see someone but she'd refused so he'd blown it off and simply put up with her behavior. Maybe if he'd insisted, if he'd done something, none of this…

"We need to start thinking about arrangements," Brian said in a thick voice, cutting into his thoughts.

Alan's head snapped up, his arms rested on his thighs. "You're right. And we need to think about the press as well. They'll be all over us until this is settled."

Brian uttered an expletive. "Vultures."

"Alan why don't you stay with us tonight," Stacy said. "You shouldn't be alone and we are family."

Alan nodded. He knew he couldn't stay in this house knowing what had happened here. He didn't know if he'd ever be able live here comfortably again—another thing he'd have to consider once everything was settled.

The detective returned. "We're finished here. The medical examiner is going to take the body. You'll need to come down to the morgue to sign some papers."

Alan swallowed. "Okay."

"Sorry for your loss," the detective murmured and walked away.

One by one everyone filed out, leaving the saddened trio alone. Stacy got up to look out the window. There were still a few straggling reporters hanging around. She shut the drapes.

"I'll ride with you over to the medical examiner's office," Brian said.

Alan nodded, still numb. He simply wanted to wake up and have this all be a bad dream. Then he would have the chance to go back and fix everything that was wrong. Of course that was impossible.

"I'm going to go up and change and then we can leave if that's all right. I want to get this over with."

"Sure," Brian said.

Alan walked up the stairs to the bedroom at the top of the staircase. He dreaded going in there and when he did his insides dropped. The center of the bed still held the indentation of where Adrienne had been, her scent mixed with something old still hung in the air. The medical examiner had taken the bottles of pills as evidence. Her slippers sat neatly by the side of the bed; her favorite silk robe was draped across the bottom of it.

His throat clenched and his eyes burned. "I'm so sorry, A. I'm sorry, baby. I should have done better by you." He sunk to his knees and wept.

# Chapter 14

Dominique woke up the next morning and the first thought on her mind was Alan. The realization made her both happy and sad. Happy to think of him yet saddened by his circumstances.

She puttered around the house, fixed a light breakfast and took a shower. All the while the phone call she planned to make was dancing around in her head. What would she say, how would he sound? Would she get to speak with him at all? Would she dare leave a message if she didn't?

Entering the bedroom from her shower, she checked the clock on the nightstand. It was 10 a.m., it would be after midday back East. She crossed the room to her bed and sat down. She stared at the card with his number. She reached for the phone, hesitated, then punched in the numbers before she lost her nerve.

The phone rang four times. She was just about to hang up when a heavy male voice came on the line.

"Hmm, hello, I was hoping to speak with Alan Conners."

"Who is this?"

"Dominique…Laws."

"Dominique, is this really you?"

"Alan?"

"Yes…"

Her heart rushed to her throat. All the lines she'd rehearsed in her head went flying out the window.

"Um, how are you Dominique? I…saw all the stuff on the news. I'm really sorry."

How could he even think about her when he had so much to deal with, she thought, snapping out of her daze. "Please, I can handle it. I hope," she laughed lightly. "I called because I saw on the news about…your wife. I can't tell you how sorry I am."

"It was definitely a shock to everyone. Thank you for your concern. Really."

"If there's anything that I can do, please…"

"Thank you, I'll remember that. And, um same here."

An awkward silence hung between them then they both spoke at once.

"You first," Alan conceded.

"I just wanted to say that I'm sorry. And hopefully the next time you're out on the West Coast maybe…"

"Maybe what?"

"Never mind. It was a silly idea."

"Silly ideas have born great ideas," he teased. "Tell me what were you going to say?"

She ran her tongue across her suddenly dry lips. "Maybe when you're back this way we could…I don't know, maybe have coffee or something." She squeezed her eyes shut realizing how utterly stupid that sounded, especially now.

"I'd like that," he said, surprising her. "Why don't you give me your number?"

She did.

"Now, how are you, seriously?" he asked.

"Other than feeling as if I've been run over by a speeding train, I'm fine. It's all been a rude awakening on many levels."

"It's the one drawback of fame," he said thoughtfully, "at any given time your entire life, all the intimate, ugly details, can get splashed all over the news and twisted into any shape they want."

"I know that all too well," she said.

"Do you have any plans?"

"What do you mean?"

"About your marriage? Forget I asked that. It's none of my business."

"I don't mind telling you. I'm actually meeting with my lawyer either later today or tomorrow. I don't want to drag out the inevitable any longer than necessary."

She could hear his doorbell ring in the background.

"That's probably Brian," he said. "I'd better go."

"Sure."

"Thanks again for calling. I really appreciate hearing from you."

"You take care of yourself. Good—"

"Dominique…I, uh, definitely plan to take you up on your offer of…coffee."

Her heart pounded then settled. "I look forward to it. Take care." She hung up the phone before she said anything really silly.

When she set the phone down she realized her hands were trembling ever so slightly and she felt warm from the inside out. Her thoughts went on a sudden wild spree imagining being in Alan's presence, talking with him, touching him, looking into his eyes, seeing his smile. All without the encumbrances of spouses.

Then a pang of guilt jabbed at her. How selfish was that. He was in the throes of burying his wife and she was thinking about getting involved with him. She shook her head at her own foolishness. What she needed to be focused on was herself and getting extricated from her trifling husband so that she could move on with her life—whatever it might become. Then, maybe, just maybe, she could think about Alan Conners beyond a brief phone call of condolence.

\* \* \*

Alan walked out of the small home office, the vaguest hint of a smile on his face. Dominique. She was the last person he'd expected to hear from. He was deeply touched by her thoughtfulness with all that was going on in her life. But somehow he knew that was the kind of person she was, one who thought about others before herself. He clenched his jaw. Clifton Burrell didn't deserve her but rather deserved whatever was coming to him. He tucked his cell phone in his pocket and went to answer the door. He had every intention of seeing Dominique again. Fate had interceded. Soon they would both be free and then he could find out for sure if what he was feeling for her was real or simply an illusion. He intended to find out.

"What took you so long?" Brian asked stepping inside.

"Sorry I was, um, in the bathroom." For some reason he didn't want to tell Brian about his call with Dominique. It seemed out of place and if he was honest with himself, he didn't want to share that with anyone, not even his brother-in-law.

He handed Alan a manila envelope as he passed him in the doorway.

"What's this?"

"Came by express mail this morning. It's the contract with Howard and Stevens, all signed and sealed."

Alan took the envelope. "I'll put it in the office. How ya doing today?"

Brian shrugged. "Listen, there's something I want to talk to you about. Probably something I should have told you a long time ago."

Alan frowned. "What…about the deal?"

"No, about Adrienne."

"Oh…" His brows jerked upward. He walked into the living room and sat down. Brian paced for a few moments before finally taking a seat opposite him.

Brian leaned slightly forward and folded his hands in between his parted thighs. "I thought she was better." He raised his head and focused on Alan's perplexed expression.

"Better? What are you talking about?"

Brian's clasped hands tightened. "When we were growing up, I guess A was about twelve when she started having these—" he shook his head, as if searching for the word "—episodes."

Alan's insides shifted. *Episodes.*

"One day she would be almost deliriously happy, on fire, couldn't sit down. And the next she was practically morose. That went on for about a year or two. My folks attributed it to moving into her teens and hormones. As she got older she seemed to, I don't know, control it better. But she would always drive herself. She had to be the best, the prettiest, the smartest, the hardest worker and then she would sink into periods where she wouldn't get out of bed. I know for a fact that she tried to…hurt herself. My folks thought I didn't know, but I did. They hid it when they rushed her to the hospital, said it was food poisoning." He shook his head. "It wasn't. When I went in the bathroom after they'd taken her to the hospital every pill bottle in the medicine cabinet was empty."

Brian drew in a long breath. "By the time you and I met she seemed to be better. I didn't know if she was on some kind of medication or if whatever it was had passed. My parents never talked about it and took whatever they knew to their graves and, of course, A never said a word."

He looked across at Alan. "Did she ever say anything to you?"

Alan slowly shook his head. He shot out a short dry laugh. "I called them episodes, too." In a distant voice he told Brian what he'd been dealing with over the past few years, how Adrienne had seemed to grow worse. But he never thought she would do something like this or else he wouldn't have ever left her alone.

"It's not your fault. Adrienne knew she had a problem. At some point she probably came off her medication and that's when things began to escalate. You couldn't have known."

"I tried to get her to go to a doctor, but she refused. I should have forced her," Alan said, guilt clutching him by the throat.

"I stayed up all night last night thinking about her, how tortured she must have been," Brian said.

"Thinking about all the things I should have done, what I might have seen but ignored. Hindsight is always twenty-twenty."

The two friends sat in silence, wrestling with their consciences.

"Maybe she's finally happy," Alan said in a faint voice.

"Yeah, maybe." He looked at his friend. "It couldn't have been easy for you."

"It wasn't. Believe me. But most of the time she was okay," he said, needing to reassure him, take some of the weight off of him.

"Well," Brian said on a deep sigh. "We have some plans to make. Stacy is making calls."

Alan nodded.

Soon this part of his life would be over, he thought. A part of him that he'd shared with someone else was no more.

"Come on, let's go see this man. I want to make sure that she looks beautiful," Alan said.

# Chapter 15

Clifton unlocked his desk drawer, took out all the documents he needed and shoved them into his portfolio. He had a two o'clock flight and he didn't want to get held up with any technicalities. He turned on his computer and downloaded his files onto a zip drive before wiping the computer clean.

It was apparent that Dominique had no intention of coming back. If she did, she would have shown up by now. She'd really surprised him. He was sure she couldn't hold out this long without him. Maybe she was tougher than he thought. None of that mattered now, anyway.

He hadn't heard anything from Manny who had

refused to return any of his calls. That was fine, too. He did a last-minute check of the office, making sure he wasn't forgetting anything or leaving something behind. Satisfied, he headed out.

Clifton stood in the doorway and looked around at the house for the last time.

He remembered the day he and Dominique had moved in. They were so happy. She was so happy.

Dominique had turned to him in this very doorway, her face glowing with elation.

"We did it, baby, we did it!" She wrapped her arms around his neck and kissed him tenderly on the mouth. "I love you," she whispered. "With all my heart."

At that moment, the only thing that mattered to him was keeping that look of joy on her face.

"That's all I want for you," he said. "The world is yours and I'm going to make sure you get it."

And he had. His every waking hour had been devoted to "making" Dominique Laws a household name, a star. He pushed and kicked open doors, spent hours negotiating, hunted down the best deals for her. At times he thought he was more concerned with her success than she was. Dominique didn't have to lift a finger. Before she could think of it, he'd taken care of her every need. The only thing she had to focus on, he repeatedly told her, was her career.

"You do the acting and I'll take care of the rest."

Sometimes you can do your job too well, he mused as he shut the door and walked to his car. As time moved on and the roles kept coming in and her star rose higher, he began to diminish. He tried to remember when he first realized the tides had shifted.

They were attending some awards dinner and the paparazzi were out in full force. Dominique was glowing that night, radiant.

A reporter jumped in front of them and snapped their picture. "Mr. Laws, how does it feel to have such a successful wife?"

Clifton's gut clenched. *Mr. Laws?* "Who wouldn't feel great having a wife like Dominique," he'd said, tossing off the slight with a glib remark.

They made their way inside the amphitheater and found their seats, but he couldn't shake off the unsettling sensation. Although polite he was unusually quiet that night. And when they returned home, Dominique, still high on the events of the evening, wanted to make love. For the first time in their relationship Clifton didn't see her as his wife and lover but as some entity, something greater than himself, this icon, this star. And all he had become was husband to the star.

Something changed in him that night and it only grew worse as articles from time to time would appear referring to him as *Mr. Laws*. Dominique didn't seem to notice or if she did, she didn't care. But it festered inside him like a cancer, growing, eating away at his feelings for her until he became vindictive.

He supposed that's when the affairs began. Being with other women who fawned over him gave him back the machismo he felt he no longer had with his wife. At least with other women he wasn't blinded by the brilliant light of *the star. He* was the star.

Clifton took one last look at the house before pulling off. Well, he'd taken her down, back to earth with the rest of the mortals. Now she would know what it felt like, what he'd felt like for so long, what it was to be insignificant.

He drove away and knew he'd never come back.

Dominique waited near the window for Manny to arrive. He'd called shortly after she'd spoken with Alan and told her he'd set up an appointment with a divorce attorney. "He comes highly recommended," he'd advised her.

She didn't know what she would have done these past weeks without Manny. He'd been her rock, the thing her husband should have been.

Her heart ached when she thought about Clif. She knew things had been strained between the two of them, but never in her wildest dreams had she imagined that it would have come to this.

Manny told her that Clifton contacted him several times wanting to know about her. Dominique was adamant about not letting him know anything. She didn't want to risk talking to him and giving in to his smooth talk and his charming ways. Clifton had the innate ability to make you believe whatever he wanted you to believe. In time, he would be able to convince her that what she had seen in her bedroom was not what she'd thought she'd seen at all. That's how good he was. It was that skill that had made him so successful as her manager all these years.

They'd worked so well together. Right up to this moment she still could not understand what changed him, what changed them.

She heard the car pull up in front of her house. She peeked out the window. It was Manny. She popped a mint into her mouth, got her purse and jacket and walked out.

"Percy Silver is one of the best," Manny was saying as they pulled off. "He's hard-nosed but discrete when necessary. He's worked with some of the biggest names in the business."

Dominique nodded, but didn't respond.

He thought he caught the faintest scent of alcohol. "Are you okay?"

"Fine. I guess. This is a big step."

"Are you sure this is what you want to do?"

"Yes," she said unequivocally. "I just want it to be over as soon as possible so that I can move on with my life." She stared out the window. "Has he called again?"

"Not in a few days."

"Hmm."

"At least the papers have latched on to a new story," he said. "Damn shame about Conners' wife."

She swallowed. "Yes, I saw it on the news."

"But once it gets out about your divorce, you will be back front and center."

Her head snapped in his direction. "I thought you said this guy was discrete."

"*He* is, but the media isn't. There's always someone digging for a story. It's bound to come out. You need to prepare yourself for that."

Life would be so much simpler if she were just a regular person, she thought. At the very least her personal life wouldn't interest the entire world. Manny was right, all the discretion in the world wouldn't keep the media from sniffing around. Once the divorce was final it became public domain.

At this point she no longer cared. She simply wanted out. She wanted to put her life with Clifton behind her no matter how much it hurt. What had gone so wrong? The question continued to haunt her. They'd been so happy once. At least she thought they were. But Clifton changed. It was subtle at first, but then had become outright cruelty. She had no clue as to what she'd done to deserve his disdain.

"Here we are," Manny said, breaking into her sobering thoughts. He turned to her. "You okay?"

She nodded her head. "Let's get this done." She opened her door and got out.

"It's a pleasure to finally meet you," Percy said, extending his hand when Dominique walked into his private office. "Sorry it's under these circumstances. Please have a seat."

Percy Silver was the poster boy for the suave attorney. His suit of steel gray easily cost five grand or better. His Hollywood tan was impeccable, making his coal-black hair, midnight blue eyes and sweeping brows stand out. He was tall, athletically built and moved with the assuredness of someone used to getting his way.

"Let's get right to it," he said, unbuttoning his jacket and sitting down behind his desk. He pulled out a yellow legal pad. "How long have you been married, Ms. Laws?"

"Please, call me Dominique. Ten years."

He wrote that down then looked directly at her. "Who controlled the assets?"

"Clifton took care of everything, the bills, the payments, the bank accounts."

He pursed his lips. The hint of a shadow passed over his face. "What do you want to get out of the settlement?"

"I don't want anything. He can have the house, the cars. I only want what's mine."

"I assume you were married in California."

"Yes."

"And you understand that under California law your assets are his assets—community property— and if he chooses, he gets half…of everything."

"But he cheated on me," she said in her defense.

Percy nodded. "That may be true, but he is still entitled to half. All the money that you earned during your marriage he can sue for half. I'm not saying he'll get it, because I'll work my ass off to make sure that he doesn't, but it could get ugly. There's no telling what his defense will be."

"The woman got on national television and told the world she had an affair with my husband and that she was pregnant with his child," she said in utter disbelief.

"I know," he said somberly. "I saw the news." He paused. "I'm sorry. Manny told me that you haven't been home for nearly a month."

She glanced away.

"He could easily counter-sue for abandonment. I know it sounds crazy, but in my line of work I've seen and heard it all." Percy took a breath. "I'll file the papers today and I will make sure that they remain sealed. Adultery and irreconcilable differences."

"Fine," she said weakly.

"I'll need to get some financial information from you so that we can begin to secure your assets until the case is adjudicated."

He asked her some more questions about her accounts, the value of the house, what other property they owned.

"Okay." He looked at her with a smile, putting down his pen and pushing his pad to the side. "I'll get started today. And in the meantime, I advise you not to have any dealings with him, do not contact him except through me. I'm sure once he is served, he'll bring his own lawyers in and we'll be the ones to get dirty in the trenches." He leaned over, pulled open a drawer beneath his desk and took out some papers. He reviewed them for a moment before handing them over to her. "I'll need you to sign these giving me permission to review your assets." He pushed the papers across the desk and showed her where to sign. She did so and handed them back. Percy pressed the intercom. "Connie, can you come in for a minute?"

Moments later Percy's legal assistant, Connie, stepped into the office.

"Yes, Mr. Silver."

He ripped off the second sheet from his legal pad and handed it to her. "I need you to start working on these financials as soon as possible."

"Sure, I'll have a prelim by this afternoon."

He grinned. "That's why I love ya."

"Show your love in my bonus." She winked and walked out.

Percy returned his attention to Dominique. "We've been working together for more than fifteen years," he said, by way of explaining their light-hearted bantering. "Good to have people you can depend on."

Dominique thought of Manny.

"Well, that's the first step." He patted his desktop with both hands for emphasis. "Next I'll get the papers drawn up, filed and delivered."

She thought she'd feel relieved that this first hurdle was underway, but the only emotion she experienced was apprehension. In truth, this was only the beginning. And knowing her soon-to-be-ex husband the way she did, he would be tenacious to the very end.

Dominique stood. "Thank you. I really appreciate you taking this on."

Percy flashed his megawatt smile. "It's what I do." He came around the desk and escorted her to the door. "I'll be in touch."

Dominique stepped out into the waiting area where Manny was perusing a magazine. He looked up when she approached and dropped the magazine onto the glass tabletop. He stood.

"So, how'd it go?"

"Well, since I have nothing to compare it to, I think it went fine."

They walked together to the elevator and rode down in silence.

Once they were back in the car, Manny couldn't refrain from asking what had been on his mind since they'd left her house.

"Dom, have you been…drinking again?"

Her entire body stiffened. "Just a glass of wine before we left to calm my nerves. I was nervous." She practically pouted.

Manny eased out of the parking lot. "Dominique, I know you've been through a lot. But you can't fall back, not now. You have to remain clearheaded."

"One drink of wine is going to fog my brain?" She sputtered a caustic laugh. "Come on, Manny, be for real."

He concentrated on the road. "One drink will lead to another. That's what I'm worried about."

"Don't be. I'm a big girl. I'll be fine."

"You need to consider therapy, Dominique."

"No! And I don't want to discuss it again." She stared out the passenger window, signaling that particular topic was finished.

"Fine," he said on a sigh. "Anything you need before I drop you off?"

"I don't think so." She was sure she'd used enough mouthwash to erase any scent of the three glasses of wine she'd had. Strangely enough she didn't feel a thing, almost as if she'd grown immune to its effects. But she'd needed something. Between talking with Alan and knowing that she had to face an attorney to talk about ending her marriage, her nerves had begun to unravel. In the future, she'd simply have to camouflage it better. She turned to him, her voice softer. "I'm sorry. I had no right to snap at you after all you've done. But I'm fine, really I am. It was only one drink." She patted his arm then held it. "You do believe me don't you?"

He turned to look at her and saw exactly why Dominique Laws was a great actress.

# Chapter 16

"I'd like you to come into my office," Percy said into the phone a week later.

"Is everything okay?" Dominique asked.

"I'd prefer we talk about it when you get here," he said.

Dominique had a bad feeling but she wasn't going to let it get the best of her. "Fine. I can be there in about an hour."

"Good. See you then."

Percy stared down at the documents in front of him and thought about how he was going to break the news to Dominique.

Dominique paced the small space of her home,

chewing on her thumbnail. What could Percy want and why couldn't he tell her on the phone? A sick sensation took hold of her stomach. This couldn't be good.

She needed a drink. That would cool her out. She hurried to the kitchen and took out a bottle of wine she had hidden under the sink. Taking a glass from the cabinet she poured the liquid until it almost reached the brim.

For a moment she stared at the glass. It seemed to be calling out to her. Her conscience nudged her. She knew she shouldn't. But her will was weak. *Don't!* one half of her mind screamed. The other said, *one little drink won't hurt.*

She put the glass down. Then snatched it up, shut her eyes and swallowed until it was drained.

Her heart thundered. The rush flowed through her. She drew in a long breath and opened her eyes. Slowly, she put down the glass, straightened her shoulders and prepared to leave.

By the time she arrived at Percy's office, the slight buzz had worn off. She checked herself in the rearview mirror, took a mint from her purse and popped it in her mouth. As she rode the elevator upward, she repeated to herself like a mantra that whatever Percy had to tell her, she could take it. She could take it.

Percy was standing inside his office door when she got off the elevator.

"Dominique." He stepped out and walked toward her. He put his arm around her shoulder. "Come in.

Connie, hold my calls." He escorted her into his office. "Please sit." He shut the door and went to his desk.

Dominique settled herself into the chair, placed her purse on her lap and folded her hands tightly on top of it.

"I'll get right to the point." He flipped open a leather-bound folder then looked directly at her. "Clifton has wiped you out."

Her mind froze. Whatever he'd just said wouldn't process.

"He's emptied the bank accounts. The house is in his name, not yours, along with the cars. The stocks have been cashed in." He closed the folder. "Other than your clothes, the one car you have and whatever you can salvage from the house—that's it."

She couldn't breathe. Her lungs had stopped working. Her head pounded so violently she couldn't hear whatever nonsense this was he was talking. Broke. Wiped out. It couldn't be. This was someone else's nightmare. No, it was hers, the very same nightmare that had awakened her on more nights than she could count.

"He's cancelled your credit cards. There was one small savings account that apparently he didn't think of or had forgotten. You have a grand total of nine thousand dollars."

Her hands started to shake even as she squeezed the life out of her pocketbook.

"Dominique?" He peered at her.

She had yet to utter a word.

"Do you understand what I'm telling you?"

She blinked several times. Her lips trembled as she tried to form words. In slow motion she rose, turned like an automaton and walked out.

Percy jumped up from his chair, rounded his desk and went after her.

"Dominique." He grabbed her shoulders and turned her around. The vacant look in her eyes threw him back on his heels. "Come back inside."

She shook her head. "I need…to leave…now," she said in a monotone. "I'll call you tomorrow." A smile reminiscent of a weak lightbulb framed her mouth.

"Let me call Manny."

"No. I'll be fine." She gently removed his hands from her shoulders and walked out.

Percy hung his head. This was going to get really bad. He returned to his office and immediately called Manny.

Somehow Dominique found her way back to her car. She felt as if she were functioning outside of her body, watching someone else walk in her shoes. But this was her life, her very broke, busted and disgusted life.

Anger, rage, fury and frustration began to simmer. She got behind the wheel of her car and sped out of the lot. She raced through the streets, tearing around slow-moving vehicles, zipping through yellow lights and nearly causing several accidents in her wake.

By the time she reached her home the simmer had bubbled to a boil. She stormed into the house, outrage fueling her blood. She screamed and screamed until her throat was raw even as she picked up anything within reach and threw it, crashing lamps, picture frames, dishes and glasses against the walls. A cry so painful and so deep that it rose from the very bottoms of her feet rushed upward and burst through her lips like a volcano—hot, devastating and searing, leaving her weak and trembling.

Through the haze of her fury she looked upon the destruction she'd created as she crumbled to the floor amidst the debris that had become her life.

She curled into a fetal position on the floor and sobbed until her eyes were totally drained of tears and her insides tender.

The phone was ringing and wouldn't stop. She managed to flip over onto her back, stare up at the ceiling. What was she going to do? How was she going to live? Between the scandals and the snubs from studios there was no immediate work in her future. What was worse, now she couldn't even afford to pay for a divorce to get away from that bastard husband!

She started to laugh at the absolute absurdity of it all. But there was no one to blame but herself. She'd been a fool all these years, allowing emotion to overrule common sense. She had no clue about her own finances and was totally in the dark about where the money was kept or how it was spent. Clifton had been responsible for everything. She'd left it all up to him. She'd never questioned him as long as her credit cards worked when she used them and the lights came on when she threw the switch. Now she was paying for her naïveté.

Dominique made it to her hands and knees and pushed herself up. She stumbled into the kitchen, again ignoring the incessantly ringing phone. She opened the cabinet beneath the sink and took out her wine bottle finding it almost empty. *Figures.* The irony wasn't lost on her.

She turned around in a slow circle, walked back into the front room and got her purse. She had about one hundred dollars in cash. She walked out, got in her car and drove away.

"Hey, aren't you that actress, um, Dominique Laws, right?" the clerk behind the counter said. His eyes shown brightly.

"Can I have two bottles of scotch, please?" she asked.

He pointed a finger at her. "You are Dominique Laws. Wow! Right here in my store. Wow."

Dominique fought hard to keep from screaming. She adjusted her dark glasses on the bridge of her nose.

He turned behind him to pick out her request. "Having a party?" he asked, putting the two bottles on the counter.

"How much?"

"Oh, I get it. You're being incognito!" He chuckled at his presumed insight. He lowered his voice. "Hey, it's on the house." He put the two bottles into a plastic bag. "Come back anytime."

She snatched up the bag before he changed his mind. "Thank you," she murmured, turned and hurried out.

The sun was beginning to set by the time she returned home. She went inside and locked the door. She flopped down on the couch with her package on her lap. After a bit of effort she got the first bottle open. For a moment she stared at the warm golden brown contents and seemed to see her life floating around inside the bottle. She brought it to her lips and took the first burning swallow. Her throat burned, her eyes teared, but the next one went down smoother, and the next and the next.

The banging and pounding penetrated the haze. She blinked but the room wouldn't come into focus. When she moved her head, the room moved with her. She groaned. The banging continued, followed by shouts of her name. Her head felt like it would explode.

She pressed her hands to her temples.

"Dominique! Dominique! Open the door. It's me, Manny! Open the door." Bang, bang, bang.

"Go away," she groaned, her voice traveling no further than a foot in front of her.

"Dominique, I have management with me. If you don't open the door on your own, I'm going to let them use the key and come in."

She closed her eyes. *Whatever.* She couldn't get up even if she wanted to.

The door opened and sunlight streamed into the room, nearly blinding her. She covered her eyes with her arm.

Manny stepped inside. "Thank you," he murmured to the man behind him. He shut the door and looked around, not believing the destruction in front of him. And in the middle of it all sat Dominique, curled up on the couch with two empty bottles turned over on the table in front of her.

Manny approached and sat down next to her. He snatched her arm away from her face.

"What are you doing to yourself?"

"Go away, Manny," she managed to say.

"That's what you want, to be left alone to wallow in self-pity? That's not the Dominique that I know."

"You don't know me. You only know the image."

"No, I know you. And you're better than this. You can't let him do this to you."

She turned bleary, bloodshot eyes on him. "He's already done it. Or didn't you get the memo? He's taken everything. I have nothing. I have no money, no career, no husband, not even my dignity if the press has anything to do with it. I can't even afford my attorney!" She started to laugh.

"Don't worry about Percy. I'll take care of it."

"I can't let you do that."

"I'm doing it and it's settled. But that's not what concerns me. You concern me and what you're doing to yourself, which is far worse than anything Clifton can do to you." He waited a beat. "You need help, Dominique. Real help."

She lowered her head. "I want to get out of California. Away from the lights, the memories, the prying eyes."

"And go where?"

"Home to Atlanta."

## Chapter 17

Dominique knew her sister Annette wasn't thrilled to have her back in town again. But staying with her sister was only going to be temporary, Dominique reasoned as she walked through the airline terminal to the passenger pickup area.

After her last binge, Manny insisted that she come and stay with him and his wife. She didn't have the strength or the will to resist him so she gave in. After a month of them hovering and asking her every few hours if she was all right, it was slowly starting to drive her a little crazy. She debated the benefits of going back to Atlanta, especially to stay with her sister, whom she knew harbored some irrational resentment toward her. It wasn't the best of situations, but at least she would be on familiar ground and maybe by some miracle she and Annette could patch up the big hole in their relationship.

She wove her way in and out of the throng of travelers and walked toward the down escalator. Annette had agreed to meet her at baggage claim. Dominique glanced up to check the signs.

"Dominique?"

She looked behind her to the line of people going up on the escalator. A man who was almost at the top was waving. Alan?

She got off at the bottom and looked up. He'd turned around and was coming back down. Her heart was racing like crazy. Alan.

"Hey," he greeted, his smile was like a warm blanket wrapped around her.

She looked up into his eyes and sunk into their depths and didn't want to ever emerge. "Hi."

"What are you doing here? Traveling?"

"Um, I'm going to be staying with my sister for a while."

"Really? Wow, that's great." He studied her expression. "Isn't it?"

She gave a tight smile. "Depends." She laughed outright. "My sister is interesting, to say the least."

His gaze ran over her face like a tender caress and she would have sworn under oath that his hands followed every place his eyes landed. "Are you here to meet someone?"

"Actually, I have a flight to catch. I'm going out to the coast. I thought I would take you up on that offer of coffee." He grinned.

"Guess that will have to wait until you get back," she said softly.

The overwhelming desire to take her in his arms and crush away all the pain and uncertainty he saw in her eyes was so strong that he couldn't stop himself as he leaned down and kissed her. His eyes drifted shut for an instant as the first moment of contact flowed through him like fire.

He stepped back, stared at her slightly parted lips for an instant. Everything around him seemed to shrink into the distance. All he could see was Dominique.

"I won't apologize," he said, his voice thick. "I think I've wanted to do that since the first time I saw you."

Dominique's knees felt weak. "When will you be back?" she said on a breath.

"Two weeks."

She nodded slightly. "I'll be here."

"You still have my number—call me," he said, almost sounding urgent. This time there was no hesitation, no doubt. He clasped the back of her head in his hands and pulled her to him, kissing her long, deep and slow.

Alan stepped back. "I'll see you in two weeks."

All she could do was bob her head. He got back on

the up escalator, holding her in place with his gaze until he reached the top and was sucked into the crowd.

Dominique touched her lips, still tingling and sweet from his kiss. She glanced up needing some kind of sign that what had just transpired wasn't a dream. But there was nothing but surge upon surge of unfamiliar faces. Yet, her heart still thundered, her blood still ran hot. She knew it was real.

Drawing in a long breath of hope and anticipation, she turned with a bounce to her step, more sway in her hips and a secret smile on her mouth as she walked to meet her sister.

She spotted Annette almost instantly. For a moment she waited and watched her sister from behind a pillar.

Her compact body was taut as usual, the energy behind her small frame barely contained. She paced, alternately checking her watch against the arrival board on the wall. Her dark, probing eyes searched the countless faces. Her expression shifting like a cloud moving across the sky from open and inquisitive to dark and angry then back again.

Dominique and Annette were as different as any two sisters could ever be both in physiology and temperament. Annette was no more than five feet five with heels, all hips and tits, as the guys used to say as she'd swing by them on the streets of Atlanta. Dominique, on the other hand, was tall and statuesque, five nine in her bare feet, well-proportioned but not overindulged. Annette was the color of smooth dark chocolate, whereas Dominique took her coloring from her great-great grandmother, a Seminole Indian, her skin the color of cinnamon, her hair jet black, her eyes dark and stormy. Annette blamed the world for her ills, both real and imagined. She lived her life as if the weight of right and wrong had been heaped on her shoulders. But rather than rise to the challenge, she was resentful and angry. Dominique lived her life believing in the goodness of others and that openness had afforded her one opportunity after the other, fueling Annette's resentment of her beautiful sister.

Finally Dominique made her appearance known. Annette's eyes widened momentarily—in that instant, Dominique almost believed that her sister was happy to see her. Then just as quickly the tight seal on her lips and the downward turn at the corners halted any chance of a smile.

Dominique walked forward, pulling her one carry-on behind her with a pinned smile of greeting on her face. "Hi, Annette. It's really good to see you." She bent down and kissed her sister's cheek.

"The car is in the lot. I waited so long for you that I wound up parking," she said instead of hello. She hung her bag on her shoulder and began marching off like a commander leading her troops.

Something akin to misery settled in the pit of Dominique's stomach as she took her place behind her sister and followed her out to the parking lot.

"I made up the guest room for you," Annette was saying, as they drove out of the airport. "Nothing fancy, nothing like what you're used to," she added. "But it's clean and comfortable."

"I'm sure it's fine, Ann, and I appreciate it."

Annette stared ahead. "All that stuff in the papers, true?"

Dominique chuckled sadly. "Which stuff? There's been so much lately."

"About Clif and that woman?"

Dominique swallowed. "So she says."

"Hmph, damn shame." She tossed a quick glance in her sister's direction. "You'd think that with all that money, fame, pretty hair and all, a man wouldn't want to look at anybody else."

The barb stung just as it was intended. Dominique looked out the window.

"How long you planning on staying?"

"Not long," she struggled to stay.

"Hmm."

Annette opened the door to her modest two-bedroom home. After her divorce from Stan Hastings she got the house and the car. Stan was just happy to be out of the marriage and left with one suitcase and the clothes on his back. There were times, when the couple was still together and Dominique was still living in Atlanta, that Stan would confess how unhappy he was with Annette. Nothing he did could please her and when she found out she couldn't have children, her disposition hardened even more. But he stuck it out for twelve years until he couldn't take it anymore. Neither she nor Stan ever understood why Annette was so miserable.

"I guess you remember where everything is," Annette said, tossing her bag on the living room couch. "Make yourself comfortable." She walked off, leaving Dominique standing alone.

Dominique drew in a breath and debated the wisdom of her decision to stay with her sister. As soon as she could, she would try to find someplace else to stay, but that would take money—money she didn't have.

She went up the short staircase to where she remembered the guest room to be and opened the door. The single bed was covered in a flowered bedspread, white curtains were hung across the window. A dresser with a twelve-inch television on top were the only other furnishings. She sat on one side of the bed and opened her suitcase, taking out her clothing and putting them away.

She went to stand at the window, which looked out onto a small garden, and was surprised to see Annette out there tending to the flowers. As she watched Annette take such tender care of the blooms, she saw a side of her sister that Annette never revealed. She seemed gentle and soft and Dominique's heart clenched at the realization. For all of Annette's hard-edged bravado, she was terribly unhappy.

Dominique let the curtain fall back in place. She wished there was some way she could reach Annette, but her sister never allowed her to get that close. There were countless invisible barriers all around her and from the outside looking in that's the way Annette wanted it.

Well, since she had to stay here, Dominique made up her mind to be as unobtrusive as possible.

For the entire flight, all Alan could think about was seeing Dominique and knowing that when he returned to Atlanta she would be there. He knew that legally she was married and he would still have to tread lightly. But her shamble of a marriage wouldn't deter him from seeing and talking to her as much as she would allow.

In a twisted way, perhaps both Adrienne and Clifton had handed them a second chance. If Dominique would give him an opening, he knew that could make something magical happen between them. He felt it as surely as he felt the beat of his heart.

That kiss at the bottom of the escalator still lingered on his lips and on his mind. If how it made him feel was any indication of what it would be like to totally have her as his own… He sighed heavily. Heaven help him.

He glanced out the window as the clouds raced by and couldn't wait to get back home.

## Chapter 18

Dominique and Annette kept a comfortable distance between each other, making polite conversation when necessary. But beyond that they functioned almost like strangers instead of flesh and blood.

Dominique hadn't ventured out much beyond Annette's home. She wasn't quite ready to deal with a public that might recognize her.

One morning while Annette was at work at the local social security office, Dominique was in the kitchen fixing something to eat when her cell phone rang.

The instant she saw the number, her pulse raced. "Hello."

"Dominique, its Alan."

Her eyes brightened and a smile bloomed across her mouth. "Hi," she said on a breath. She draped an arm around her waist and leaned against the counter. "How is your trip going?"

"Everything went fine."

"Went?"

"Yep. I tied everything up and I'm back in Atlanta. Got in last night. I would have called then, but I didn't want to wake you."

"You could have called."

"I'll remember that next time." He paused. "So… how is everything going? You getting settled?"

"As settled as I can be, I suppose."

"Are you free later or do you have plans?"

"Um, I don't have anything special planned."

"Great. How about lunch?"

"Sounds wonderful. What time?"

"Two, if that works."

"Sure. Um, where did you want to meet?"

"Do you remember your way around?"

She laughed. "Pretty much."

"Then can you find your way to Gladys Knight's place? Best chicken and waffles in the state."

She heard the laughter in his voice. "I'm sure I can find it."

"So I'll see you at two."

"I'll be there."

"I'm looking forward to it. Bye for now."

Dominique took in a long breath and slowly exhaled. She squeezed the phone to her chest and shut her eyes as she allowed the excitement of the moment to flow through her. When she opened her eyes they landed on the clock hanging on the wall above the fridge. It was only ten-thirty, but it was never too early to start getting ready.

She darted upstairs to her bedroom to look through her meager belongings in the hopes of finding something appropriate to wear.

Funny, this moment reminded her of her youth, going on a first date with a guy she really liked and trying to find just the perfect outfit. Back then she didn't have much either, but she made do and she was happy, really happy with her simple, stress-free life.

Surely her fame and money had afforded her much over the years, but what had she sacrificed as a result? In truth, she'd sacrificed a life. Simple things like going to a movie, sitting in a restaurant or going to the supermarket turned into events. Every time she stepped out of her door she had to remember that she was Dominique Laws and the world expected her to be polished and perfect 24–7.

Yes, she'd enjoyed the benefits of celebrity: getting the best seats, invitations to *the* parties, the freedom to travel. But there were many nights that she longed for the simple life she'd had here in Atlanta, when she could go out without makeup, her hair in a ponytail, and simply walk along the streets like everyone else without worrying about her picture being taken or people rushing up to her for an autograph or an interview.

Maybe now she could get that part of her life back, some semblance of normalcy.

As she hunted through the closet, her cell phone rang again. Her first thought was that it was Alan calling to cancel and her spirits slowly sunk until she spotted the number on the lighted dial.

She depressed the talk button but didn't say a word. She waited.

"We need to talk, Dominique."

She swallowed over the knot in her throat and willed her heart to slow down. "I have nothing to say to you, Clifton. Talk to my lawyer."

"Dominique, I'm sorry…for everything. You didn't deserve what I put you through."

She frowned with confusion and apprehension. Clifton Burrell didn't apologize—ever.

"You cheated on me, you let me see it! You wiped me out, humiliated me in public and you're sorry," she asked incredulously her voice rising in pitch. "Yes, Clifton you're exactly right, you *are sorry.*" Fury pounded in her temples. "There's nothing you can say to me. Not now."

"I still love you, Dominique. I always have."

He actually had the nerve to sound sincere. Who was the real actor in the relationship?

"There's so much I need to tell you. Let me come

and see you, wherever you are. I'll come. We can talk. Just talk, that's all."

Her will wavered ever so slightly. His voice sounded like the Clifton she'd known and fallen in love with, not the critical, unbending man he'd become.

"I can't do that."

"You can if you want to," he cajoled. "Please."

She gripped the phone until her fingers ached. "Goodbye." She disconnected the call before he could react. The phone rang in her hand. This time she refused to answer. She tossed the phone on the bed as if it were contaminated. She watched it shimmy across the comforter until the ringing finally stopped.

The call shook her. The last person she'd expected to hear from was Clifton. She was sure he was off on some island somewhere enjoying his spoils.

The anticipation she'd had only moments ago had been dashed with icy water.

What could he possibly have to say to her? *I still love you, Dominique. I always have.* When was the last time Clif had said he loved her? She couldn't remember. Those were words that she'd desperately needed to hear, but he had refused to say them. As if by withholding his words and his affections he could control her emotions as well. And he had.

She drew in a breath. She wasn't going to let his call ruin her day. Then he would have as much control as he always did. She turned back to the closet, glanced over her choices and made her decision.

* * *

Not wanting to get lost and needing to give herself plenty of time to get to downtown Atlanta, Dominique prepared to leave the house with a good hour to spare.

She was turning the knob on the door to go out when it was pushed in from the other side.

"Oh!" they said in unison as Dominique took a step backward.

Annette walked in looking her sister up and down. "Going out?"

"Yes, I have a lunch date." She smiled.

Annette arched a brow. "Date? Whether you accept it or not, you're still a married woman," she said with as much cynicism as she could summon.

"I'm aware of that, Annette. It's lunch. No more, no less."

"Hmph, that's how it always starts." She turned her back and walked away.

Dominique rolled her eyes and walked out.

The last thing she'd wanted to do was ask to borrow her sister's car, but without a vehicle, she had to rely on mass transit, which was a brand-new experience for her. The last time she'd been on a bus or train was nearly fifteen years ago. The ride on the bus to the rail system did give her a chance to get a look at Atlanta. Not much had changed since she'd left, other than there seemed to be many more people, businesses were thriving and everyone looked to be driving an expensive car.

As she gazed around at all the faces that looked like hers she realized how much she missed being here, having roots, friends, belonging to a community. Sure, actors were in a community of their own, but they lived in the upper stratosphere of life removed from the day to day. They had the money to pay people to do day to day for them.

She got off the bus at her stop then took the short train ride to downtown. After several wrong turns she finally found her destination.

She pulled open the door and walked into the cool, dimly-lit interior. She took off her dark shades.

"Good afternoon and welcome. How many for lunch?" the hostess asked.

"Um, actually I'm meeting someone."

"Oh, wonderful. Let me check the book." She went behind the podium and opened the reservations book. She glanced up at Dominique. For a moment she hesitated as if recognition was trying to push its way to the surface. "Name of the party?"

"Conners. Alan Conners."

The hostess's face brightened perceptibly. "Oh, Mr. Conners. Yes, he arrived about ten minutes ago. I'll take you to his table."

"Thank you." She followed the bouncy young woman around the tables until they came to a private booth in the back, shielded from the rest of the patrons by a frosted glass partition.

When Dominique came around the partition and

saw him, her heart immediately began to race. Her face grew so hot she thought she'd started sweating.

Alan stood with the most welcoming smile on his face and in his eyes as she slid into the booth seating opposite him.

The hostess handed her a menu. "The waitress will be over to take your orders shortly."

They barely acknowledged her. All of their attention was on each other.

"I'm so glad you came."

"So am I."

"Have any trouble getting here?"

"No."

He reached across the table and took the tips of her fingers in his hands. An electric sensation scurried up her arm. She nearly shivered with delight.

"I haven't stopped thinking about you, Dominique," he said in a voice so totally intimate that it reached inside her and caressed her soul. His eyes played with every nuance of her face. "I know it sounds like a line and it's probably totally out of place, but it's true." He flashed a lopsided grin. "It's making me crazy."

"I haven't stopped thinking of you, either," she confessed.

"I know this is a difficult time for you and I'm not going to put any pressure on you. But I want to see you as much as I can, as much as you'll let me."

His comment rushed the conversation with Clifton to the forefront of her thoughts.

"Dominique?" He peered at her. "Something I said?"

She blinked and focused on him. She shook her head. "No. I'm sorry. It's not you. I got a call this morning." She looked at him. "From my husband." She saw him flinch.

"I see." He released her hand.

She snatched his back. "Please, it's not like that. It's just that when you said the thing about this not being an easy time…it made me think of the call, that's all."

"Did he say something to upset you?"

"I suppose if you call telling the woman you cheated on and stole from that you still loved her is upsetting, then yes, he did say something upsetting," she said a bit more harshly than necessary.

"I'm sorry. I shouldn't pry."

She sighed. "You're not prying and I don't mind talking about it. Maybe talking would help." She gave him a soft smile.

For the next two hours they shared stories of their marriages, the good with the bad, how it had affected them, the reasons why they chose to stay, even knowing why they should go.

"Guess we were both pretty stupid, huh?" Dominique said as she cut into her waffles.

Alan shrugged slightly. "I wouldn't say stupid. Love and obligation will make you do crazy things. I think both of us remained tied by obligation and duty more so than anything else."

Dominique chewed thoughtfully. "That's true. I know I felt that I owed Clifton everything, my very existence." She pushed out a sigh. "If it wasn't for him I'd probably still be waiting tables right here in the ATL." She chuckled sadly.

"I firmly believe in the order of things." Alan steepled his fingers and tucked them beneath his chin. "Everything in life happens for a reason and when it's supposed to. Moments like this are a perfect example."

She angled her head to the side. "Moments like this?"

"If neither of us had gone through what we did, met the people who came into our lives, traveled the roads we did, you and I would never have met. And if we had, it would have been the wrong time. We wouldn't be ready and we wouldn't be who we are right at this moment."

She'd never really thought about it that way. A smile of acceptance moved across her mouth. "It does make sense. Life is a journey." She reached for her glass of water. "I guess we can even thank Adrienne and Clifton for screwing with our lives."

Alan snorted a laugh. "Yeah." His expression sobered. His gaze pulled her to him. "So whaddaya think? You think the stars have finally aligned?"

"I think they're heading in the right direction." She pressed her lips together in thought, then spoke. "What's next for you?"

"Good question. Well, Brian and I just closed a

deal on some major funding to get our production company up and running."

Her eye widened in awe. "Your own production company. Oh, my goodness. Congratulations."

Alan beamed. "Yeah, we're pretty thrilled."

"Where are you going to be based, here in ATL?"

"We thought about it. It's a toss-up between here and New York. Both are ideal locations and in dire need of what we can offer."

"Wow," she breathed. "That is so exciting."

"Even with the funding, it's still going to take us at least six months to a year to get up and operational."

She nodded. "But you're so close."

He grinned. "Yep. I can taste it. How long do you plan to stay in Atlanta?" He'd reached across the table again and was playing with her fingers while she spoke.

The tingling in her hands and arms made it very difficult to concentrate on something as simple as breathing in and out, let alone answering questions.

"Um, I'm not really sure. I'm kinda rootless at the moment."

"I know it would cause all kinds of scandals, but you could always come stay with me…if things get too…uncomfortable with your sister."

Dominique's face heated. "Alan…I…"

He held up his hand. "Just a suggestion, a pretty over-the-top one, but just a suggestion." He leaned closer and lowered his voice. "Although having you at home with me is very tempting and to hell with the scandals."

She lowered her gaze. "Easier said than done." She shook her head ever so slightly. "I thought I'd developed a tough skin over the years. I mean in this business there will always be critics and gossip. But—" she looked upward for a moment "—I never thought I'd be at the center of a firestorm. I didn't fully appreciate how vicious the media could be."

"I don't know how you all do it. I mean practically having to live your life surreptitiously just to keep the press off of you."

"It's not always as wonderful as people think."

"If you could be anything you wanted, what would it be?"

"Hmm."

She tugged on her bottom lip with her teeth and to Alan it brought to mind the action of a young girl, innocent and carefree—the Dominique he caught flashes of when she let her guard down.

"To be honest, just a regular girl." She laughed lightly. "Don't get me wrong, I love what I do. But sometimes I wish I had a life like everyone else." She focused on him. "What about you?"

"I want to be a great filmmaker, someone whose films make a difference and are remembered. I've never wanted anything else…other than a family of my own."

Her heart knocked. Her gaze darted around before settling back on him. "Clif never thought it was the right time for kids," she confessed. "In hindsight maybe it was a good thing we never had children."

"I think you would make a wonderful mother."

She smiled sadly. "As they say, the old clock is ticking. I think my time has passed."

The waitress reappeared with their check. "Can I get you anything else?" She looked from one to the other.

"No. Nothing for me," Dominique said.

Alan took the check and pulled out his wallet and credit card. "Thanks, the food was wonderful." He handed the bill and the card to the waitress.

She stared at Dominique for a moment. "I, um, hate to be rude, but aren't you that actress that was on the news recently?"

Alan answered for her. "Yes, you are being rude." He flashed her a hard look and she slinked away, mumbling her apologies.

Alan turned to Dominique, who looked as if she wanted to disappear. "I'm sorry about that."

"It's not your fault. No need to apologize."

"Listen, do you have plans for the rest of the day?" he asked.

"Nothing special."

"Good, then you can spend it with me. If you want to," he added quickly.

"I'd like that."

They spent the rest of the afternoon wandering around the city, sharing stories about their childhood experiences, how the city had changed and grown.

He stopped at an outdoor flower shop and picked out a single yellow rose and gave it to her.

"Something rare and beautiful just like you."

She felt her eyes well with tears. It seemed like forever since she'd heard such sincere kind words. Her emotions were so fragile that the bold act of gentleness broke her into little pieces.

"I'm sorry," she said, lowering her head.

Alan tilted her chin upward with the tip of his finger, compelling her to look at him. "You have nothing to be sorry for," he said gently. "You've been through a lot."

She sniffed and blinked back her tears. Alan reached out and wiped them away with the pad of his thumb. The touch was electrifying. She all but trembled beneath his simple touch. His smile was soft, his gaze inviting. She could feel the warmth of his body envelop her. The air between them was charged. She held her breath. They were so close.

It took all he had not to kiss her. He inhaled her scent and the hair on his arms rose. He tucked a strand of hair behind her ear that had been blown loose. She clasped his hand to her cheek and held it there. For an instant she closed her eyes and pretended that all this was okay, when inside she knew differently.

She opened her eyes and drew in a short breath. "I better get back."

"I'll drive you home."

They walked back to his car that was parked in the lot of the restaurant. While they walked their fingertips would intermittently touch or their hips would bump as they sidestepped pedestrians. The stroll back to the car was more sensual than foreplay. Dominique had to concentrate on putting one foot in front of the other and not the steady beat between her damp thighs or the fact that her nipples had grown so hard they rubbed against the inside of her bra every time she moved, setting off a series of tiny shockwaves.

As he helped her into the car his body brushed up against her and they both felt the energy surge between them. Her glance shot over her shoulder to land on his face. Raw hunger burned in his eyes. His nostrils flared ever so slightly as if he couldn't get enough oxygen. Dominique looked away, her heart beating madly in her chest.

Alan got in behind the wheel and gripped it so tightly the veins in his hands pulsed. He stared straight ahead as he spoke to her.

"I'm going to say this because I have to. I want to make love to you Dominique. Right now."

The confines of the car grew smaller with every breath she took.

"I know you're still married. And I know Adrienne has only been gone a short time, but the reality is you're here and I'm here. In the eyes of the world it would be ugly and wrong." He turned in his seat to look at her. "But quite frankly, my dear, I don't give a damn," he said, borrowing the famous line. He blew out a long breath of air. "So, now that you know how I feel, whenever you're ready…" He let his offer hang in the air and they drove off.

## Chapter 19

Annette heard a car pull up into her drive and went to the window to look outside. She watched her sister in close conversation with a man. Her ire rose. She'd barely been in town a month and already she'd found someone. Probably bartered on her looks and notoriety, she thought, the old jealous demon rearing its ugly head.

All their life it had been Dominique that the boys would go after. It was Dominique who got the second looks, the second dates, the relationships, the success. She, on the other hand, was stuck raising her after their mother died. She was the one who had to quit school and get a job, put food on the table and clothes on their backs. All Dominique ever had to do was be pretty.

She let the curtain fall back in place when she saw Dominique turn out of the intimate embrace and walk toward the house. Didn't she have any self-respect? She was still a married woman. No wonder her husband ran around on her. Annette huffed into the kitchen just as the front door opened and shut.

"Annette!" Dominique called out. She walked through the living room toward the sound of banging cabinets in the kitchen. She stood in the doorway. "Hi. You're home early."

"Didn't expect me to be here, I suppose." Her tone was decidedly snide.

Dominique frowned in confusion. "You usually get home after six, that's all." She stepped into the room. "Is everything okay?"

Annette whirled around, her expression a roadmap of hard lines. "I should be asking you that." She planted a hand on her hip.

"What is wrong with you?"

"Wrong with me! I wasn't the one practically undressing on my front lawn."

"What?"

Annette spun away, her anger bubbling over. "Maybe that kind of stuff flies back in L.A. where everything goes and everybody is sleeping with whomever. But it doesn't work around here."

"Annette, have you totally lost your mind?"

"I put up with you as a kid because I had no choice. But I damned sure don't have to do it now. And if you can't respect my house, then you can get out."

Dominique blinked rapidly in disbelief. "You want me to leave?"

Annette drew in a breath. "I don't know why you picked me instead of one of your high society friends."

"You're my sister," she said softly. "I thought if I could turn to anyone, it would be you. I guess I was wrong."

Annette stared at her, tight-lipped. She lifted her chin in challenge. "That's all I was ever good for, someone to come to when the going got tough."

"I never thought that."

"You didn't have to. It was obvious."

"What have I done to you, Annette, to make you resent me so? It's been like this between us for years."

"Look at you. Look at you. You have everything. You always did. The looks, the personality. Everything just fell in your lap. You never had to work hard for anything. I was always the one in the background. And when you made it big, did you ever think of me? Of course not, not until you needed something."

"Don't blame this on me. Don't you dare. You never made it easy to have a relationship with you no matter how hard I tried. I thought you were glad to be rid of me. Anytime I called you were always busy and couldn't talk. I never got a response to any letter I sent, any card." She swallowed. "So I gave up trying."

"Do you know what it's like to have to give up your life for someone else and never have one of your own? When Mom died I *had* to take care of you. I gave up my dreams for you. And never once did you ever say 'thanks, sis.' Never." She slowly shook her head. "I don't even tell people that we're related. They'd never believe me. Look at me and look at you," she tossed out as an accusation. "I'd open a magazine and there you were. I'd turn on the television and there you were. I'd go to the movies and there you were, basking in all your glory and success." She snorted her disgust.

"You have no idea what my life was like, Annette. You say I don't know what it is to give up my life for someone else." She smiled sadly. "You're so very wrong."

The two sisters faced each other.

"If you can give me a week or two I'll find someplace else to stay."

Annette folded her arms. "Fine," she managed.

Dominique looked down at the floor. "Fine." She turned and walked out.

She went up to the spare bedroom and slumped down on the bed. She had never understood her sister's resentment toward her. Finally it was clear—plain and simple jealousy. Annette got it fixed in her head that Dominique always had it easy, that she didn't have to work for what she got. Nothing could be further from the truth. Annette was ten years older than her. Annette was seventeen when their mother died from a drug overdose. Annette always tried to make it seem like it was something exotic—that their mother *passed away*. The truth was, Amy Laws was a heroine addict who died in a drug den with a needle in her arm.

She barely remembered her mother and what she did remember wasn't pretty. In her young mind she thought that life would finally be good after their mother died, they'd take care of each other. But that was not the case. Dominique didn't know which was worse, finding her mother in the bathroom all doped up or taking the verbal and emotional abuse from her sister—who seemed to blame all of her woes on Dominique. Over time she made herself immune to Annette's slights. She stayed quiet and out of her way.

Dominique looked around the room. Where was she going to go? She certainly didn't have enough money for a hotel and until the investigation into her finances was complete, she had no income. Nine thousand dollars wouldn't take her very far.

Her cell phone vibrated then rang. She picked it up and checked the number.

"Hello?"

"I know I just left you, but I wanted to tell you that I really enjoyed myself."

She closed her eyes and relished those words. "I needed to hear that."

"What's wrong? I hear it in your voice."

"Nothing for you to worry about. I can handle it."

"Dominique, don't hesitate to call me, for anything. I mean it."

"I'll remember that."

"I have a couple of appointments tomorrow during the day, but if you're free tomorrow evening, I thought we could have dinner."

She tried to swallow the knot building in her throat. "I— I'd like that."

"Great. I'll pick you up around seven."

"I'll be ready." She hung up the phone, holding on to Alan's voice and his words as long as she could before confronting her current dilemma. What was she going to do?

Alan had debated about calling Dominique. He knew how bad it would look for her to be seen with him so soon after Adrienne's death and with her impending divorce. It all boiled down to pure fodder for the tabloids. The one fortunate thing was that this was not L.A. where they would be hunted like rabbits on Easter Sunday. For the most part, the folks here minded their own business. That's what he would bank on.

The anticipation he felt about seeing her again was like the feeling a teen gets on his first date, pure nervous excitement. He knew that Dominique had a lot to deal with and overcome. The months ahead were going to be difficult at best. He wanted to be there for her as much as he could, as much as she would allow.

It had been so long since he'd felt this strongly about anyone. Being with Dominique opened him up again to feeling, to caring, to wanting to love. The years he'd spent with Adrienne had their good moments, but overall it was emotionally draining. He wanted to feel again and he knew deep in his soul that he could with Dominique.

Alan walked into his study and sat down behind his desk. He took out the contractual agreement—his new lease on life. In the next few weeks, he and Brian would meet with the architect to design their offices. Tomorrow he and Brian were scheduled to meet to work out a leasing deal for the equipment they would need for their new studio.

His pulse quickened. Everything he'd ever dreamed of was coming together. By this time next year he would be head of his own studio, calling the shots and making the kinds of films he wanted. His thoughts drifted back to Dominique. He would make a film just for her and put her where she belonged—on the screen, back on top.

The following morning Percy walked into his office but came up short when he saw the its-not-good-news look on his secretary's face.

"Come on in and let me have it," he said breezing by her without stopping. He walked into his office and dropped his briefcase on top of his desk. He unbuttoned his suit jacket and stood waiting for whatever was coming his way.

"I finished the paperwork on the Laws file."

"Uh-huh."

"It's not good. Apparently, Mr. Burrell has done a major disappearing act. Whatever he took from the missus he took with him, lock, stock and barrel. I'm sure he's on some island somewhere out of our jurisdiction."

"I figured as much. So trying to recover any of her money is out of the question." He pushed out a breath. "I'll proceed with filing for the divorce. Abandonment and adultery. In the interim I need you to get in contact with the D.A. I want him to initiate charges of theft and fraud against our Mr. Burrell. At least that way we won't have to worry about him returning to muck up the divorce at the eleventh hour. If he's that foolish, his ass will not pass Go and head straight to the big house."

"I'll take care of that right away."

Percy gave a short nod then turned to look out the window. He slid his hands into his pants pockets. It was a smog-filled California day. The tops of buildings and the mountainsides beyond were barely visible. Somewhere way out there, Clifton Burrell had disappeared and had taken with him everything that his wife had earned over the years. According to bank statements, what he hadn't taken he'd spent.

In all the years that he'd been an attorney, it never failed to amaze him how despicable people could be to each other, especially people who'd vowed before God to do right by one another. Those were usually the worst.

He turned away. All he could do was try to make as much right out of the wrong as possible. In this case the best he could do was to permanently sever Dominique's ties to her husband. It was going to cost a pretty penny. Fortunately, Manny was footing the bill. It was a dirty job, this divorce business, but somebody had to do it.

## Chapter 20

Dominique and Annette had not spoken since their falling out. Dominique had stayed in her small room until she'd heard Annette leave for work the following morning. Her dreams had been plagued with the nightmare that had always haunted her—*losing everything.* But what troubled her even more was the rift between herself and her sister and she didn't know what to do about it.

How much of a role did she really play in Annette's feelings of worthlessness? Perhaps she could have tried harder to forge a relationship with her sister. It was true that she'd become consumed by her career on the runway and then on the screen.

But Annette for all of her blustering and hard edges was always the take-charge one, the one to depend on to get things done. Annette acted as if she enjoyed telling others what to do and when. They'd easily fallen into their roles and it had shaped the people they'd become. Unwittingly, Dominique had grown comfortable—too comfortable—with someone always taking care of things for her. She'd become a lifetime dependent—ultimately to her downfall. Annette may not have had a life of glitz and glamour, but she'd held fast to her independence and her strength.

She loved and admired her sister, but she'd never let her know how much; she'd simply taken it for granted that Annette could handle anything.

Dominique walked to the window and looked out into the morning. It was past time that she took control of her own life and thanked Annette for providing the pathway that had made her life possible.

It was a new day, she thought, an opportunity to do things differently. She went to the dresser and took out her journal. It had been a while since she'd opened the pages and jotted down her thoughts. She took the book and curled up on top of the covers.

She flipped through the pages and memories of her life bloomed before her; the fear and excitement she felt on her first modeling job and the celebration with Clifton afterward; making the covers of *Elle* and *Vogue*; her first screen role, her engagement and marriage, her first Golden Globe nomination and her Golden Globe win. All of the milestones in her life were carefully documented. The pages vibrated with energy and images.

Dominique turned to a blank page and began to write. The words and emotions flowed onto the paper as fluidly as the ink. She wrote about her marriage, the highs and the lows, her feelings of isolation from the world and the loss of her sense of self. She described in detail the pain and sense of betrayal that she felt when she discovered Clifton's infidelity and her descent into the bottle to dull the hurt and confusion that she'd experienced. And in the midst of it all there was a glimmer of hope and expectation—Alan. His appearance in her life at that precise moment and time came when it was supposed to, even though they were both married to other people. They were destined to meet and find a way to each other through all the obstacles of their circumstances. She believed that with all of her being.

Alan was like a lightening bolt, a brilliant flash in the heavens that left all who saw it in awe each time he came in contact with you.

Once her divorce was finalized she would be totally free, no regrets, no looking back and then she could fully explore all of the possibilities with Alan. She only hoped that her growing desire for him wouldn't outrun her better judgment.

Dominique closed the journal and returned it to

the dresser. She had plenty of hours to kill before meeting Alan, so she decided to do something special for her sister.

She took a quick trip to the local grocery store and while she was waiting in the checkout counter line she noticed two women in front of her who kept looking over their shoulders at her and whispering to each other. She shifted her weight from left to right and inched up the line growing increasingly uncomfortable. The two women paid for their purchases and walked out, intermittently glancing back over their shoulders.

When Dominique got in front of the cashier her heart pounded against her chest. There on the front page of the *National Enquirer* was a picture of her at the Golden Globes and beside it a picture of her when her photograph was snapped in the doorway of the motel. The caption read One-time Film Star Crashes and Burns. There was a smaller picture of Marcia talking about her and Clifton's "love child."

Dominique felt ill. Blindly, she paid for her purchases; all the while the cashier kept staring at her. Dominique hurried outside, feeling as if she was walking along the streets completely naked with the whole world watching her. She kept her head lowered and barely missed smacking into another pedestrian. She made a turn at the corner and spotted a liquor store. Her stomach jumped in anticipation. She hesitated while running her tongue over her lips. Annette didn't drink, so there was nothing in the house stronger then Diet Coke. Dominique looked around, clutching her purchases to her chest. *Just one little bottle of wine.* Before she could change her mind she hurried in, bought a bottle of white wine and came right back out.

Her plan was to make a wonderful meal for her sister as a small way of saying thank you and hopefully providing a bridge between them.

She took out the chicken breasts and began seasoning them. The bottle of wine, still in the brown paper bag, whispered her name. She turned to look. Her mouth watered. She put the chicken breasts on the nonstick pan, placed the prepared stuffing she'd bought on top, then rolled the chicken, sealing the stuffing inside. She washed her hands. *Just one little sip.* The images of those two women and the picture of her on the cover of the *National Enquirer* loomed before her. Swiftly she crossed the room and snatched up the bag with the wine.

She pulled the bottle from the bag. It definitely wasn't of the quality she was used to. She didn't need a corkscrew. This bottle had a twist-off top. She glanced around the room as if expecting someone to walk up behind her and demand to know what she was doing. She brought the bottle to her mouth and took her first swallow in more than a month. The liquid was like fire going down her throat. She shuddered. A moan slipped through her lips. That first drink was like being touched by a man in the most intimate of places for the very first time and knowing instantly that it couldn't stop there.

With as much willpower as she could summon, Dominique lowered the bottle to the table and wiped her mouth with the back of her hand. The bottle sat on the table in slender accusation. She turned back to the stove, switched on the oven and slid the pan with the chicken onto the rack. She still had the vegetables to prepare and the rice. But her throat ached for another swallow, just a little one.

She retrieved the bottle from the table and took it with her to the living room.

That was the last thing she remembered until the piercing sound of the smoke detector penetrated the fog along with the violent shaking on her shoulder.

She opened her eyes to see nothing but fury on Annette's face. The room was heavy with smoke and the scent of something burned beyond recognition. She tried to push herself up to a sitting position and the entire room shifted with the effort.

"What the hell is going on? Get up!" Annette dashed into the kitchen and started opening windows.

Dominique groaned. She pressed her hands to her head to stop the pounding. She looked around. A layer of smoke hung in the air. What had happened? She spotted the empty bottle of wine on the coffee table. She groaned again.

Stumbling to her feet she got up and went into the

kitchen. Annette was bent over the stove pulling out the tray of charred meat.

"You could have killed yourself and burned down my damned house!" she shouted before tossing the pan and its contents into the sink.

"Annette...I'm so sorry. I..."

Annette whirled on her. "I want you out. Not in two weeks—tonight. You can't stay here." She ran water over the pan and another plume of steam rose, the sizzling sound as chilling as Annette's ultimatum.

"I don't have anywhere to go."

Annette faced her, her expression unrelenting. "I don't care."

Dominique lowered her head, turned away from the destruction she'd caused and went upstairs.

Oh, God, how could she have done this? she thought. Maybe Manny was right, maybe she did need professional help. She packed her few belongings, took a quick shower and changed her clothes. It was almost six-thirty by the time she was finished. Alan would be there to pick her up shortly. Maybe he could take her to a hotel.

She took her suitcase and her purse and went downstairs. Annette was still in the kitchen cleaning up Dominique's mess. Dominique stood in the doorway, not daring to enter.

"Annette, I'm really sorry. I never meant to cause you all this trouble. I wanted to make dinner for you and..."

"And you decided to get drunk instead," she snapped not bothering to look at her sister. "All the tabloids were right about you."

Dominique flinched. "I'm going." It was barely a whisper. "I promise not to bother you ever again."

Annette's back stiffened, but she refused to turn around.

Dominique sighed heavily, turned and walked out. She opened the front door and shut it softly behind her; she walked the three steps to the bottom of the stairs and sat down to wait for Alan.

*Chapter 21*

When Alan pulled up in front of Annette's house, he was surprised to see Dominique sitting forlornly on the steps. He got out and the moment he looked at her and saw the suitcase at her feet he knew something was terribly wrong.

He sat down beside her. She looked at him, her eyes shimmering with unshed tears.

"Tell me about it in the car," he said gently. He put his arm around her and helped her to her feet.

She leaned her weight against him as he led her to the car and helped her in. He tossed her suitcase in the backseat, jumped behind the wheel and took off.

Dominique sat pressed to the door, her fist against

her mouth. She didn't utter a word, but Alan caught glimpses of her wiping away tears. He desperately wanted to ask her what had happened, but he feared if he did she would completely fall apart.

Instead of going to the restaurant he'd selected, he headed home. The last thing Dominique was in shape for was being out and around a lot of people. He pulled into his driveway. Dominique didn't even acknowledge that they obviously weren't at a restaurant.

Alan got out of the car, came around and opened her door. She looked up at him through red-rimmed eyes. He took her hand and she grasped it like one grabbing hold of a life preserver.

"Let's get you inside," he said gently.

Numb, she nodded her head and got out of the car. He took her suitcase from the backseat and led her inside.

When she walked into Alan's home an overwhelming sense of safety engulfed her. The warm colors, the simple and unobtrusive decor lent itself to serenity.

Alan walked into the living room and set her suitcase down near the couch. He turned to her. "I'm sure you don't feel like talking or explaining. Whenever you're ready, I'll listen," he said. "And you can stay here for as long as you want."

Tears welled in her eyes and flowed over her lids and down her cheeks. Alan came up to her and drew her close. She wrapped her arms around him and buried her face in his chest.

He held her like that for what seemed like a blissful forever, tenderly muttering words of comfort while stroking her back and her hair.

Then without warning the dam broke and she wept, crying tears of loneliness, hurt, fear, confusion and gratitude. Her body shook with the force of her sobs but Alan didn't let her go. He held her tighter, assuring her that everything would be okay. Whatever he needed to do to make it okay, he would.

"I feel like such a fool," she managed to garble, her voice a thread thin.

"We all do at some point," he said, stepping back slightly to look down at her. His statement brought a shaky smile to her lips. She sniffed hard.

He brushed her hair away from her face. "And then we get over it and move on."

She drew in a breath and moved out of his embrace. "Some days I feel like it will never get any better. The instant I see daylight another storm is on the horizon."

She wandered over to the couch and sat down as if she balanced the weight of the world on her slender shoulders. Alan came to sit next to her. He put his hand on her thigh.

"I didn't mean for it to happen," she said, her voice coming from some distant place. The vision of Annette's face, the acrid smell of smoke filled her, the realization that it could have all turned out even more tragically caused her to tremble.

"You didn't mean for what to happen?"

Slowly she began to recount the events of the day, what happened at the supermarket, her breaking down and buying the bottle of wine, the smoke, Annette putting her out.

For several moments Alan didn't speak, wanting to be sure he found the right words. The picture of her standing in that hotel door flashed in his head. So it wasn't an isolated incident, he concluded. It was her crutch, a crutch that would do her more damage than if she let it go and fell as a result. He knew all too well the damage and despair that alcohol could cause. He'd seen its insidiousness up close and personal with his father and what it had ultimately done to his mother and the family. Dominique could get past it and beat it if she really wanted to. But she had to want it more than anything and no amount of pushing and shoving would help.

"I'm not going to sugarcoat anything. I'm pretty sure that's not what you want to hear or need to hear. The truth is you could have been seriously hurt." He saw her recoil. "I don't agree with what your sister did, no matter what her reasons. When someone is hurt and in trouble you don't turn your back on them." He thought of Adrienne and how his inaction may have led to her suicide. He wouldn't sit back and let something like that ever happen again to anyone he cared about. He cupped her chin and turned her to face him. He looked deep into her eyes. "We'll get through this, together. I'll give as much as you do and more for as long as you want."

"I just want to be happy," she said.

He caressed her cheek with the tip of his finger. "And you will be. I promise." He kissed her lightly on her forehead. "Let me show you around and get you settled then, if you're up to it, we can fix something to eat."

Alan showed her the ground floor and the back-yard of his house before taking her up to the bedrooms and study. He opened the door to a nice-sized bedroom at the end of the hallway.

"I think you'll be pretty comfortable here. There's an adjacent bathroom through that door." He pointed across the room.

"Thank you." She turned to him. "I mean that."

He gave her a lopsided grin. "I know." He clasped her shoulders. "Make yourself at home," he said, emphasizing every word. "I'm a very low man on the totem pole so you don't have to worry about anyone infringing on your privacy. Feel free to go out back whenever you want."

She nodded. Her throat grew tight.

"I'll leave you to get settled. If you find you need anything, just holler. I'll be downstairs."

"Okay," she whispered.

Alan walked out, closing the door quietly behind him. Dominique took a slow turn around the room to take in her new surroundings. Sheer white curtains and razor-thin vertical blinds hung in the window that overlooked the garden in back. The gleaming wood floor was covered in the center by a brilliant mahogany-and-cream area rug. The bed dominated the room. The four-poster queen-sized bed was piled high with an assortment of pillows that spread across the bed. At the foot was what appeared to be an antique chest that gleamed as brightly as the floors. A matching dresser and chest stood on the other side of the room.

She opened the door to the bath and was tickled to see the sunken Jacuzzi tub. She smiled for the first time in hours before walking out to unpack.

After emptying her suitcase, she frowned. Where was her journal? She checked her oversized bag. It wasn't there, either. She checked the compartments in the suitcase. Nothing.

She turned slowly around. Where was it? She tried to recall the last time she'd had it. She'd been in bed. It must have fallen to the floor.

She slumped down on the bed. Every personal iota about her life was tucked away on those pages. She needed to get it back even if it meant facing her sister again.

Annette wearily climbed the stairs, having done all she could to rid her little home of smoke. She felt dirty and sticky. She walked down the hallway toward her bedroom, passing the room her sister had used on the way. The door was open, the bed unmade.

A new wave of anger bubbled and boiled to the surface. She stormed inside, her eyes racing around the room. The sooner she got every and any sign of her sister out of her house the better she would feel. She went to the bed and began stripping it. She pulled the covers off the bed and tossed them on the floor then took off the pillowcases. She was bent down to pick up the bundle when she noticed a book sticking out from under the nightstand. She crouched lower and pulled it out.

It was a thick leather-bound book, about the size of a large paperback novel with enough pages to recreate the Bible.

Annette stared at it. There was a thick latch that kept the book closed, but it wasn't locked. She pressed her lips tightly together and flipped open the cover. The first page dated back to when their mother died.

Annette's stomach clenched as she relived Dominique's life through her carefully written thoughts. She was transported through time and became intimate with a sister that she hadn't known.

Annette lowered herself and sat on the stripped bed, her eyes clouded by tears as she read the details of Dominique's marriage, her hidden fears of losing everything, the pain she felt at being estranged from her sister, the role she had to play simply to get from one day to the next. And then there were the entries about Alan Conners and suddenly all the gloom seemed to fade away. Annette instantly felt the lightness in Dominique's heart, her feelings of hope even in the midst of her personal battles.

Page after page. Some happy, some sad, some thoughtful, but all powerful and personal.

Annette's eyes burned and felt gritty. When she turned her stiff neck toward the window, she was stunned to see that dawn was breaking over the horizon.

She closed the journal. Although she'd read through the night, she felt as if she'd barely scratched the surface. She needed to find her sister. It was way past time that they crossed the bridge that had separated them for so many years.

Dominique awoke the following morning to the smell of sizzling bacon and what definitely smelled like biscuits. Her stomach hollered. She'd fallen asleep the night before on top of the covers, fully clothed, without eating a thing. The first thing she did was look wildly around her for any sign that her deep sleep was the result of another drinking binge. But as she did so, she quickly realized that what she felt was refreshed and clearheaded, not groggy and confused. A smile moved across her mouth.

She sat up and stretched every limb in her body until she heard her joints snap and pop in protest. Hoping off the bed, she ambled over to the bathroom, stripped and got in the shower. She knew if she so much as looked too long at the Jacuzzi and got in it, she would be out for the count again.

After her shower, she put on a pair of knee-length shorts and a T-shirt and went downstairs. She followed her nose to the kitchen.

Alan turned at the sound of her approach with a warm smile of welcome. When he saw her standing there, his heart thumped. He'd spent a near sleepless night knowing that she was only a room away. When he'd checked on her last night and found her curled up on the bed, it had taken all his willpower to keep from curling up next to her. He'd tiptoed inside and put a light blanket over her, kissed her tenderly on the cheek and eased out. She'd barely stirred.

"Good morning. I peeked in on you last night after you didn't come back down, but I didn't have the heart to wake you."

She grinned shyly. "I wondered how that blanket wound up on top of me. I can't remember the last time I slept that well and that deep."

"You needed it, that's all. Hungry I hope?"

She grabbed her stomach when it shouted again. "Just a little," she said with a smile.

"Great. Hope you like pancakes."

"Love them. Can I help with anything?"

"Hmm, you can take the dishes and stuff out to the patio. I thought we could eat outside."

"Sure."

Seated at the table, in the shade of a striped

umbrella, they ate a leisurely breakfast of eggs, pancakes and bacon with a side of biscuits with butter and jelly, a pitcher of orange juice and a carafe of piping hot coffee.

"I'm stuffed," Dominique finally said, pushing back from the table.

"Hope you enjoyed it," he said.

"Every bite." She wiped her mouth with the napkin. "I'll help you clean up."

They worked comfortably side by side in the kitchen as if being together in his house early in the morning were commonplace. Dominique had never felt so utterly comfortable.

"I really want to thank you for taking me in," Dominique said as she put away the last dish. "You didn't have to do it."

He leaned against the sink and dried his hands on a towel. He folded his arms. "I like having you here. The circumstances that brought you here aren't ideal, but I'm still glad you're here."

Alan extended his hand to her. "Come here," he said softly.

Dominique stepped up to him. He ran his thumb over her palm. His eyes roamed across her face. He leaned forward and lightly touched his lips to hers. She moaned softly. He pressed harder and her lips parted ever so slightly. Alan put one arm around her waist and one hand behind her head and pulled her into a deep kiss.

Lights popped behind his closed lids when the tip of his tongue connected with the sweetness of hers. He drew in the taste of her, their tongues doing a slow duel. Heat rushed to his loins and pulsed, building by degrees until he was thick and hard with need.

Dominique felt his heat surge between her legs and pressed closer to him, wanting to define his length and breadth, needing to massage her own drumbeat with a slow rotation of her hips.

Alan groaned in her mouth, grabbed her ass and pulled her as close against him as physics would allow. His mouth dropped from her lips to plant hungry steamy kisses down the short valley to her breasts. He grabbed the T-shirt from the hem and tugged it forcefully up and over her head, tossing it to the floor. For a moment, he gazed at her, watching the rapid rise and fall of her breasts, regally contained in black lace. Tentatively he reached out. His finger made contact with the silky skin. Slowly he let it travel, outlining the exposed flesh until Dominique shuddered, moaning softly.

She grabbed his hand and pressed it tightly to her burning skin. His palm covered the warm globe and gently squeezed. Dominique's breath caught in her chest then rushed out in a soft hiss.

Alan pulled the straps down from her shoulders and peeled down the cups, forcing her breasts upward in offering. He lowered his head and ran his tongue across the rising nipple. Her entire body trembled. He sucked the nipple into his mouth and played with it until she cried out, holding on to him to keep from falling. He moved to the other side and repeated the sensual ritual.

Dominique's shaky fingers found the waistband of his jeans and worked to unfasten the metal button. Before she unzipped him, she reached for the source of her desire. Taking him in her hand her eyes widened in awe at the size and how incredibly hard he was. Her heart pounded. She ran her hand up and down the length of him. He sucked a bit harder on her nipple and they both groaned in pleasure.

Alan pulled her hand away, unzipped his pants and stepped out of them, kicking them to the side. He walked right up to her easing her back against the table. The fire in his eyes left no doubt in her mind that there was no turning back.

They both took off her shorts, her beautiful body now only clad in matching black lace. Alan swiftly pulled out a chair from beneath the table. His gaze stayed glued on Dominique. He took her hand and pulled her toward him as he lowered himself down on the chair. She stood above him, her legs bracing either side of his thighs.

Alan leaned forward and with his mouth and his teeth and his fingers he pulled her thong down over her hips. Her thighs trembled. Alan pressed his face against the center of her heat. Dominique whimpered. His tongue snaked out, licking the tip of her hardened clit.

"Ohhh." Her back reflexively arched. She cupped his head.

Alan delved deeper, cupping her rear and taking her in long slow strokes that had her seeing stars. She tasted like honey, Alan thought as he suckled the tiny nub and let his tongue slip inside her opening.

Dominique clawed his hair, gritting her teeth. The sensation was a surreal series of tiny explosions. It coursed through her veins like a drug, leaving her weak and wanting. Unintelligible sounds bubbled in her throat.

Alan grasped her hips firmly in his palms and lowered her down onto his stiff penis. The initial contact stunned them both before she slowly slid down, taking him in until he filled her totally.

For several moments neither of them moved but simply held each other, relishing the newness.

Dominique let her eyes drift closed and she dropped her head to curve in the hollow of his neck. She kissed him there and felt him pulse and jerk deep inside her. She moved her hips in a slow rotation that made Alan growl with pleasure.

"You feel like satin," he whispered in her ear an instant before he surged upward. He built to a steady pace moving in and out of her like a well-oiled piston and Dominique gave back as good as she got.

She needed more of him, wanted more, deeper, harder faster. She arched her back and braced her arms on the table behind her, rocking her pelvis against him—in and out, harder and faster, teasing her clit every time she did. The electric shocks rushed through her in waves.

"Alan!" she cried.

He held her tighter as they moved in an erotic frenzy as if enough could never be enough. He cupped her breast in one hand and squeezed and released, squeezed and released. And just when she thought she couldn't stand the pleasure a moment longer, Alan slid his hand between them and fingered her clit each time she rode against him.

Dominique's mouth opened but no words, no sound escaped. The vibrations began in her legs and worked up to her thighs. He thrust deeper. She screamed. Harder. Faster. Her body convulsed in a series of mind-shattering spasms of release. Her insides gripped him, milked him until everything he felt, wanted and desired poured into her in a powerful gush.

Dominique collapsed against him. Her breath expelled in rapid bursts. A myriad of colors danced in her mind in place of coherent thoughts and her body felt as if it had been transported to nirvana.

Never in her life had she experienced an orgasm like that. It was as thrilling as it was frightening in its power and intensity. There were no words to describe the sensation that continued to pulse ever so gently inside of her.

Alan kissed her tenderly on her neck and stroked her back. He couldn't believe that after all that, sure that he'd spent the very essence of himself—he was still rock-hard and ready. He wanted her again.

Dominique lifted her head and looked into Alan's eyes. A slow smile moved across her face. "You're kidding."

He pouted and shook his head slowly. "Nope." He pushed inside her just a little to assure her that he had every intention of having her again.

"Guess what they say about older men and the one-shot deal is a lie," she murmured with a wicked gleam in her eye.

"And I'm here to prove it." He wrapped his arms around her waist and stood up, taking her with him. She giggled and wrapped her legs around him, their bodies still very much connected.

"And where are we going?" she asked before nibbling his ear.

"Someplace where I can stretch you out, lay you out and explore every square inch of this incredible body." He started for the stairs and every step caused his penis to jerk inside her and her vagina to grip him in response. The tantalizing trek from the kitchen to his bedroom was the most sensational act of foreplay either of them had ever experienced.

By the time they got upstairs and Alan kicked open his bedroom door, they were both wild with need. Hands, lips and tongues were everywhere ravishing whatever they came in contact with. They feasted on each other like warriors after a long siege.

In unison they found the perfect rhythm, flowing one into the other like musical notes on a scale. Alan was the saxophone with his long soulful strokes, each of his notes creating a new sensation, a heightened image. Dominique was the harp, graceful and elegant, her sound so exquisite it took you straight to heaven.

They played with and off of each other, building in crescendo as if an entire orchestra filled the room, their wild cries of release soaring above their notes until they crashed in an explosion of sound and sensibility.

"Yesssss, Alan… Oh, God…"

"I'm here, baby, all for you, all of it. Take it…take it…agggggh!"

The racing of their heated breaths bounced off of the walls and wrapped around them as they collapsed together in a tangle of damp limbs and deep soul kisses.

Dominique lay on her back, one leg bent at the knee, her arm draped across her waist. Alan faced her on his side, his lips pressed against the pulse that beat in her throat, his hand cupping her still throbbing sex. He slipped a finger inside the wet heat. Her hips arched in reflex. She moaned.

Alan moved his lips from her neck down to the swell of her breast. He ran his tongue in tiny hot circles around her nipple until she whimpered. He pushed his finger in and out a little faster watching her breathing escalate. She tossed her head from side to side as she raised and lowered her pelvis against his finger. Then he pushed in two. She sucked in air. Her inner thighs trembled. She spread her legs wider. He rubbed his thumb across her clit and she exploded. Her hips rose off the bed, the veins in her neck stood at attention. He felt her gripping his fingers from deep inside her womb and before her climax completed he moved on top of her and plunged deep inside her well, releasing himself in three long, hard, fluid thrusts.

Tears of elation seeped from Dominique's eyes as the ecstasy that her body had experienced began to wane. The joy of it was so sublime it was almost incomprehensible. While the act itself was so very physical, it was also more than that. She felt her soul touched by his soul. A connection she'd never before experienced had elevated what transpired between them to something akin to the spiritual.

"Something happened between us," Alan said, his voice sounding awed.

"I know. It was like I left my body."

"Yeah…that's the closest explanation."

"Kinda scary," she said with a hint of laughter in her voice.

He propped up on his elbow and looked at her. "A good kinda scary."

"Definitely."

"I could get scared like that several times a day all week long." He ran his finger down the center of her chest to her stomach.

She turned her head to look at him with an arched brow. "You are a madman," she said with all sincerity.

He winked. "Mad about you."

Dominique giggled and sighed with satisfaction. This is what she'd been missing. *He* was what she'd been missing. She'd gone through the motions with Clif, he'd shown her the ropes, but it was never this. Clif never touched her like Alan had. He'd reached inside physically, but Clif never touched her soul.

He was done. He was hooked. He was finished. His mind and body still reeled from aftershocks. Being with Dominique was beyond description. If he were to leave this world right now, he would leave it a truly happy man. He'd fallen for her, hard. The months of thinking about her and imagining her had only intensified his budding emotions. Now that he'd experienced fully loving her, he knew there was no one else for him, no one. And whatever he needed to do to ensure that they would be together, he was willing to do.

"This isn't going to be easy," Dominique said as if reading his thoughts.

"I know. There's a great big world out there that would love to gobble us up for lunch and spit us out for dinner." He pulled her closer, pressed his face into her hair. "But we'll handle it, together, me and you."

She turned on her side so they lay face-to-face. "There's some stuff that you can't help me with. I have to do it on my own."

"What stuff?"

She lowered her eyes to hide her shame. "I know I need some help…with the drinking. It was never a problem before, but it seems to be now. I don't want to resort to alcohol every time something goes wrong in my life."

"You have any ideas on how you're gonna deal with that?" he asked gently.

She drew in a breath. "I was hoping you might help me find someplace—out of the limelight." She gazed at him with hopeful eyes.

He thought about his commitment to the development of the production company and all the work that was on the table in front of him and Brian. This was not an ideal time for him to pick up and leave, but if he had to in order to see Dominique through it, then he would. Brian would simply have to hold things down.

He kissed the top of her head. "I'm…touched that you'd want me to."

"Is that a yes?"

He smiled. "Yes, that's a yes."

She released a sigh of relief while she played with his fingers. "Thank you," she said softly. "What can I do for you?" She brought his hand to her lips and kissed it tenderly.

"Girl, don't make my mind go there." He chuckled long and hard. Slowly, he sobered. "I don't want you to do anything for me except be happy, Nikki."

Her heart thumped in her chest when he called her

Nikki. It was the pet name her mother had for her before things got bad. It was one of the few fond memories she had of her childhood.

"No one has called me Nikki since I was about six," she said, her voice thick with awakened memories. Tears filled her eyes. She sniffed them back.

"Is it a bad thing…? I'm sorry…I—"

She shook her head. "No. No." She sniffed and wiped at her eyes. She sputtered a nervous laugh. "This is so silly."

"Tell me."

"My mom used to call me Nikki." Her throat tightened as she told him about her mother and the road of self-destruction she set herself on. "When she wasn't high or running behind a man, she was so funny, so loving, so beautiful," she said wistfully. "She'd sit me on her lap and twist my ponytail around her fingers as she told me stories. She told me one time that she named me Dominique because it sounded big and pretty and important and she knew I'd be all those things one day, but in the meantime the name was too big for a little girl so she called me Nikki." She laughed lightly at the memory.

"Your mother was right," he said softly.

She looked into his eyes. "I wondered several times if my…problem…was hereditary. Annette is so fearful of it that she won't drink at all for any reason."

"Good question and one that you might get the answer to when we find you the perfect place—out of the limelight. And I just want you to know that wherever it is, I'll be there with you."

Dominique pushed up in the bed. "Alan…I can't ask you to do something like that. I—"

He put his finger over her lips. "Sorry, you're stuck with me."

She drew his finger into her mouth then slowly pulled it out. "I like the sound of that."

## Chapter 22

The next few days, Dominique and Alan spent every minute with each other, talking, laughing, discovering fun facts about one another, all the things new couples do.

Dominique couldn't remember being this happy in far too long. Alan was tender and caring. He listened to what she had to say no matter how big or small. They slept late and played all day. There were no worries about what to wear, the next audition or interview, studying for a role. For the first time in years, Dominique lived like everyone else. Simply.

While they were in the middle of a late breakfast in the backyard, they heard the front doorbell ring.

Alan frowned a moment. Put his napkin down and pushed up from the table.

"Be right back." He slid open the glass doors and stepped inside.

"Where the hell have you been?" Brian demanded the moment Alan opened the door.

For an instant Alan froze. Brian was the last person he wanted to see. Since Dominique arrived, he'd turned off the house and cell phone so that they wouldn't be disturbed. Brian on his doorstep was the result.

"Oh, hey man." He gave Brian a lopsided grin.

"Hey man? That's all you have to say? I've been calling you for days. What's going on?" He tried to peer over Alan's shoulder.

"Just taking some time, that's all."

Brian looked at him curiously. "You gonna make me stand in the doorway or let me in?"

"Uh…yeah, sure. Come on in." He stepped aside to let Brian pass.

Brian came up short when he spotted Dominique standing in the patio doorway. He flashed a look at Alan.

"I'll explain…later," he said to Brian.

Alan turned and extended his hand toward Dominique, beckoning her forward.

When Dominique approached and Alan put his arm around her waist, he saw Brian's eyes cinch.

"Dominique Laws this is my…best friend and brother-in-law, Brian Chambers. Brian…Dominique."

Brian stared at her for a moment, stunned to see her in the flesh and in Alan's home. "Pleasure to meet you in person."

Dominique flashed a tight smile. "Nice to meet you, as well. Alan has said some wonderful things about you."

"We were just having a late breakfast. You're welcome to join us," Alan said.

"Um, maybe another time." He gave Alan a pointed look. "If I'd known you had company I would have picked another time to drop by."

"I can…go upstairs and get out of the way if you two need to talk," Dominique offered apologetically.

"Nikki, you don't have—"

But before he could dissuade her, she'd pulled away and was heading for the stairs.

"You want to tell me what she's doing here?" Brian hissed from between his teeth.

"If I must," Alan answered. "Come on in." He walked ahead of Brian into the living room.

Brian sat down and waited for what had to be a story deserving of *Entertainment Weekly.*

Alan sat down and rested his arms on his thighs. "We first met at the Golden Globes…"

"I don't know what to say," Brian finally murmured when Alan had finished. He looked across the short space to his friend. "She's in the middle of a big mess right now. You— We can't afford to get dragged into it. Not when we have so much going on.

If the media gets wind of this…" His voice trailed off as he shook his head. He stared at Alan. "Is this relationship worth the risk?"

"I'm in love with her, man."

Brian flinched. "What? You barely know the woman—what three, four months tops? And what about Adrienne? She's barely been buried six months and you're taking up with someone else?" He jumped up and began pacing, visibly frustrated.

"Brian, Adrienne is gone," he said softly. The words stuttered Brian's pacing. "Adrienne and I didn't have a real marriage by the end, not for a very long time. You know that. Neither did Dominique."

"So basically you're two castoffs who found each other." He tone was snide. He tossed his head back and chuckled. "That's rich. Real rich."

Alan's jaw clenched. He stood. "Look, I want to be with Dominique. Period. Whatever we have to work out, we'll work it out. And either you can be happy for me or not. That's up to you. But I'm sure as hell not going to give up my relationship because it doesn't sit right with you."

Brian gave him a hard stare. "We'll see if you feel the same way when I pull you from the deal."

Alan's eyes flashed. "What?"

"You heard me." Brian pointed at his chest. "We're supposed to be partners. We're not supposed to do anything that would jeopardize our business. This does. But you're obviously too whipped to see it." He glared at Alan. "I'm not going to let this happen. I'll find another director." He stormed off toward the door then tossed over his shoulder, "That's how I feel about your relationship." He slammed the door behind him.

Alan stood in the center of his living room in stunned disbelief. He glanced toward the door. He'd never seen Brian like that and, more important, he'd never known Brian to be so insensitive and narrow-minded. He sat down and let his eyes roam the room, searching for answers. Brian was willing to remove him from the deal simply because he didn't approve of Dominique? He was flabbergasted. There had to be more to it than that.

The two of them had worked too hard and too long for Brian to pull the plug on him. He'd contributed just as much. It was *his* talent that drew the financiers. But the reality was Brian *did* have the power to remove him from the business and replace him with another suitable director. Would he really do that? Was he vindictive enough to crush Alan's dream over his own hang-ups?

Alan glanced up. Dominique was standing in the entrance to the living room. Alan put on a good face. "Hey, sorry we took so long." He smiled and she came into the room and sat down beside him.

Alan pulled her close and sighed heavily. He kissed the top of her head.

"What's wrong?"

He angled his head and looked at her. "What do you mean?"

"I can see that something is wrong."

He lowered his gaze for a moment. "Nothing big. Just working out some kinks in the contract, that's all."

She searched his face, listened to the tone beneath the words. "If we're going to make a go of this we have to be honest with each other, even if it hurts." She waited, holding his gaze. "Deal?"

The corners of his mouth quirked upward. "Deal."

She pushed up from the couch. "I'm going to go clean up out back then I want to stop by my sister's house. There's something over there that I forgot. Would it be all right if I borrowed your car?"

"Sure. I can take you…"

"No. I'll be fine. I need to do this by myself." She started for the backyard. "Maybe when I get back you'll be ready to tell me what's wrong."

Alan watched her leave. He twisted his lips in consternation. The last thing Dominique needed to hear was that he was going to lose everything he'd worked for if he stayed in a relationship with her.

It had been a while since Dominique had been behind the wheel of a car, but it sure felt good. As she drove along the streets of Atlanta, she realized that through all the drama of the past few months things were finally beginning to mellow out. She had a man that she was crazy about and who was crazy about her. Her attorney said that barring any complications or surprises from Clifton, her divorce would be final in about another month. Manny had been faithful as always and she'd even confessed to him about her relationship with Alan. After a stunned silence, he'd actually sounded happy for her. He cautioned her to keep a low profile until everything was finalized and wanted to know when she would be coming back home.

Home. At the moment, California seemed so far removed from her reality. It was another life, a life that had nearly destroyed her. It would take a lot of hard work on her part before she could even think about going back—if she ever could. That thought jarred her. If she didn't act, what would she do with the rest of her life? The unanswered question plagued her for the rest of the trip to her sister's home.

When she pulled up in Annette's driveway her heart thudded. Annette's car was parked in front of the house. She still had her key and her hope had been to get in, get her journal and get out. She didn't want a scene.

She turned off the car and sat for a few moments, pulling herself together before she got out. She would make this as quick as possible.

Dominique walked up to the front door and rang the bell. Several moments later the door opened. Annette's dark eyes widened with surprise.

"I'm sorry to drop in on you unannounced. I left something here and I—"

"Come in." She stepped aside.

Dominique walked in not knowing what to expect. She turned to her sister. "I think it's upstairs. I'll just get it and leave." She started for the stairs.

"Wait." Annette walked past her and over to the table in the hallway. She opened the drawer and pulled out Dominique's thick journal. She held it in front of her. "Is this what you came for?"

Heat rushed to Dominique's face. She took two steps toward Annette and held out her hand.

"I. .I read it." Annette lowered her gaze, then looked at her sister as if seeing her for the first time. "I didn't know."

Dominique's lips tightened. She raised her chin. "You couldn't have."

"I've been such a bitch to you all these years— blaming you, trying to hurt you as if everything that happened to us as kids was your fault. I guess I needed to blame someone."

Dominique swallowed. "Forget it." She gave a short sad laugh. "It's all in the past."

"Not really. The past made us who we are right now." She drew in a breath and walked toward her sister. "I was so busy being the martyr and never took into account how you felt or what you were going through. I had no idea…about…Clif."

Dominique looked away.

"I'm sorry, Nikki."

Dominique's heart clenched. She bit down on her bottom lip to keep it from trembling.

"I know I can't make up to you all the crap I put you through, but I hope that we can try to at least be sisters."

Dominique's nostrils flared as she drew in air. She never thought she'd hear Annette say those words, words she'd longed to hear, had desperately needed to hear. "I'd like that…a lot." Her voice broke.

Annette wrapped her arms around her sister. They hugged and held each other, the years of detachment, resentment and jealousy evaporating like morning mist, leaving behind the bond that both of them so desperately craved.

Tears of joyous relief flowed down Dominique's cheek. She squeezed her sister to her, wanting this pivotal moment between them to last forever.

Annette sniffed, stepped back and wiped her eyes. "So you really like this guy, huh?" she said, her voice teasing and engaging.

Dominique giggled and wiped her own eyes. "Yeah, I do."

"So maybe you can invite him over so I can meet him," she asked as much as stated.

Dominique's eyes sparkled. "I'd really like that."

Annette took Dominique's hand. "I was fixing some tea. Want some?"

Dominique grinned. She hated tea. "Love some."
She clutched her journal in her hand and followed
Annette into the kitchen.

## Chapter 23

When Dominique returned to Alan's house she found him out on the patio sipping on a beer. She pulled open the sliding doors and stepped outside.

Alan glanced up over his shoulder. "Hey, babe. Been gone a while. Everything cool?" He set his beer down on the table.

Dominique beamed. "Better than cool." She pulled up a chair and anxiously leaned forward, taking his hands in hers. "I went to see Annette. Well, actually I went to get this." She held up her journal then dropped it on the table. "I'd left it at her house. She was home and…we talked, really talked." Her gaze searched the sky in wonder. "There was so much *stuff* between us, things that had gone unsaid or misunderstood for so many years. I know it's going to take time, but at least now we both want the same thing." Her smile lit up all the space around them. "I have a sister, a real sister, not one in name only." She pressed forward. "She wants me to bring you by and formally introduce you."

Alan grinned and squeezed her hand. "I'd like that." He only wished Brian felt the same way about Dominique.

"What is it?" she asked peering into his eyes.

He pushed out a breath and stood. "Nothing. Just a glitch in the contract. But nothing we can't work out," he lied smoothly.

She stared at him, hoping that he would look directly at her so she could see the truth or the lie in his eyes. He didn't.

"How 'bout a spin in the Jacuzzi?" he teased.

Dominique brightened. "Now that's an invitation that a girl could get quite used to." She slowly rose and walked up to him. She brushed her finger across his lips. His eyes raked over her.

Alan threaded his fingers through her hair. "I'm in love with you, Dominique."

The world seemed to stand still. Her chest grew so tight she could barely breathe. *Love.*

"I know I sound crazy," he stammered when she didn't respond. "It hasn't been that long—"

She stopped his words with a finger to his lips. "How

long do they say it takes to fall in love with someone?" she whispered. "A month…a week…a year…two? Or is it like magic, a moment like this when you can't explain it—you simply know it to be true."

"Nikki…"

"I think I fell in love with you the moment we met, when your hand touched mine and nothing else mattered."

"You mean that?"

"Yes. I love you, Alan."

He gazed into the deep pools of her eyes and saw the truth swimming there. He took her mouth in a sweeping kiss, the intensity and sweetness of it stunning them both. His mouth played over hers, teasing, tasting, taunting.

She sighed against his lips and sought out the hot recesses of his mouth with her tongue. He sucked it in and tiny blots of electricity coursed through her veins.

Alan pulled her flush against him so that every dip and curve of their bodies met and melded. He wasn't going to give her up, not for a job, not for a future, not for anything. He knew deep in his soul that none of it would mean anything without her in his life.

"I want to make love to you," he whispered harshly against her lips. "Slow and long."

"Just the way I like it," she whispered back.

His eyes sparked with mischief. "Last one to the bedroom has to do the dishes!"

Dominique took off like a shot, giggling all the way upstairs.

Alan caught her at the bedroom door, swept her off her feet and plopped her down on the bed. "I let you win," he said covering her body with his. He lifted her left leg to bend it at the knee.

"That's what all the losers say," she teased, laughter filling her voice.

He nuzzled the valley of her breasts. "Is that right?"

His breath was hot against her skin. She sighed in delight. "So I hear," she murmured, arching her back to give him better access.

"Let's take this to the Jacuzzi." He raised up and took her hand, pulling her to her feet. "But first…" He began unfastening the buttons of her blouse, took it off and tossed it on the bed.

She lowered one bra strap and then the other.

He unzipped her shorts.

She pushed them down over her hips and kicked them to the side.

"Your turn," he said.

Dominique's eyes darkened. She slid down his body until her face was equal with his center. Her eyes rolled up to his face while she unzipped him then pressed her lips against the hard rise in his shorts.

Alan groaned deep in his throat and grabbed the back of her head. She used her fingers to part the opening in the fabric, then stroked her found treasure with the tip of her tongue. He sucked in air through his teeth. She smiled.

He let her have her way with him for as long as he could stand it. He gripped her shoulders and pulled her to her feet.

"You made your point," he said, his voice tight. He took her by the hand and led her into the bath.

She turned on the water in the Jacuzzi and they finished undressing each other as the tub filled. She stepped in first and eased down into the hot water. Alan got in behind her and turned on the jets.

The water bubbled and fluttered around them. Dominique leaned back against Alan's chest and closed her eyes as he slowly ran his hands along her body.

Steam wafted around them.

Alan trailed his hand down from her stomach to finger her beneath the water.

Dominique sighed deeply and spread her thighs. The jet stream of the water pulsed against her sex, intensifying what Alan was doing to her.

"Hmm," Alan murmured as he slid one finger inside her. Dominique squirmed against him. He kept up his in and out exploration until he felt her entire body go rigid.

She cried out, squeezed her thighs tightly together. Alan pushed them apart and let the burst of water finish her off.

"Ooooh! Ahhhhh! Allllaan." She gripped his

knees and bucked against the water and Alan's hand, riding them both to utter bliss.

As the pulsing subsided, Dominique, totally spent and thoroughly satisfied, dropped back against Alan. She rested her head on his chest as he tenderly kissed her neck.

"Happy?" he whispered.

"Very. Very. Very."

"That's all I want—for you to be happy."

She looked at him over her shoulder then turned completely around. She rose up and straddled him. She took his face in her hands. "I want you to be happy, too," she said before dipping her tongue into his mouth and lowering herself down onto his throbbing shaft.

While Dominique slept, Alan crept from the bed they shared and tiptoed downstairs. He came down to the kitchen and took a handful of grapes from the fridge—a favorite late-night snack—then went out back.

He looked out into the night, a typical Atlanta night in June. The air was sweet, almost sticky but not quite. A light breeze barely ruffled the leaves. He popped an icy cold green grape into his mouth.

He was going to have to straighten things out with Brian, give him a chance to cool off and think things through. He couldn't believe that Brian would be so narrowminded. That wasn't the Brian that he'd known for almost twenty years. But he knew a lot of it had to do with Adrienne.

As much as Brian may have understood about Adrienne's illness and what Alan had to deal with, there was still a part of him that wanted to believe that Adrienne was the perfect wife and that Alan would never ruin that memory by loving someone else.

Alan turned his back to the night sky, leaning against the wooden railing that circled the patio. His gaze fell on the table and the thick leather journal that Dominique had left behind earlier. He took a step forward almost as if beckoned. He touched the worn leather cover and ran his fingers over the clasp that kept it closed.

He hesitated. He opened the cover. His breath shortened in his chest. Dominique's innermost thoughts were ingrained on the lined sheets.

He sat down.

Dominique awoke the next morning curled next to Alan's warm body. She snuggled closer and Alan murmured in his sleep. She turned onto her back and stretched then eased from the bed.

She went downstairs to the kitchen and poured a glass of juice then wandered out back when she caught sight of a robin lighting down on the railing. She walked toward the pretty bird as quietly as possible so as not to frighten it away.

A gentle breeze blew, ruffling the open pages of her journal and catching her attention. Her chest constricted as she realized that Alan might have read her journal. She walked over to the table and picked it up. This was the second time she'd left her journal behind. In all the years she'd been writing down her thoughts, she'd never allowed anyone to see it or even know it existed. Yet, in a matter of days she'd done it twice. The first time it was a mistake, the second time…

Maybe she wanted her sister to find her journal. Maybe she wanted Alan to find it and allow both of them to discover who she really was.

Funny it had never occurred to her to let Clifton see it. She held the journal to her chest and wondered if Alan had read any of it and if he had, had it changed his mind about her.

She whirled toward the sound of the door sliding open. Her eyes widened in question.

"I didn't read it." He stepped through the open door. "I don't want to find out about you in one big gulp. I want you to spend the rest of your life telling me all about Dominique Laws."

Her hand flew to her mouth.

"I know it's soon," he said taking a step closer. "But tomorrow or the day after isn't going to change what I know is right." He came closer. "I love you, Dominique, with all that I know and all that I can't wait to find out. Marry me and whatever comes our way, we'll deal with it together."

Her heart was pounding in her throat. All coherent thought flew from her mind.

Alan came right up on her. He curved his head to the side and looked into her eyes. "Marry me."

"Alan…"

"Just say yes. Everything else will take care of itself."

"My divorce…"

"It'll happen." He kissed her cheek. "We were meant to be together. You know that…right there." He pointed to the center of her chest.

"I um, I need to get into treatment. I…"

"I'll go with you. Next." He kissed the bridge of her nose.

Her lips trembled and she was so hot inside it felt like someone had lit a torch. "I'm an emotional wreck."

"That's what I love about you." He kissed her neck.

Her fingers entwined with his. "I…I love you." Her voice broke. She struggled to blink back the tears that threatened to spill over. "Nothing would make me happier than to be your wife."

He swept her into his arms. "You had me sweating there, woman."

Dominique laughed and wiped at her eyes. "Can't have you thinking I'm easy."

He brought her hand to his lips and kissed the back of her left hand. "We're going to have to find something perfect for that finger." His gaze connected with hers and all the love he had in his heart for her was reflected there.

"Alan, you know we can't… "

"I know, I know. But when the time is right I want something big, brilliant and beautiful."

She grinned. "But for now, it's just between me and you."

He pulled her close. "Hmm, secret lovers, I like that."

Dominique tossed her head back and laughed with all the joy in her soul.

# Chapter 24

"He's living with her!" Brian railed to his wife as he paced across their bedroom floor. He ran his hand across his head. "Adrienne hasn't been gone six months."

"Brian." Stacy got up from the bed and walked up to her husband, holding him in place with a tight grip on his shoulders. "Look at me."

He did so with great reluctance.

"Adrienne is gone. It's hurtful, it's sad, but she's gone. Alan is still here. He deserves to have a life with whoever makes him happy."

"She's still married," he countered.

"Yes, to a sleezeball." She pursed her lips in disgust.

Brian huffed.

"Is he happy?"

Brian finally focused on her upturned face. "So he says."

"Honey, who are we to judge who people should be with and how long they should mourn or when it's a good time to fall in love? Life doesn't work like that." She cupped his chin. "Look at us. Your folks hated me on sight. And my brother couldn't stand you."

He twisted his lips at the less-than-fond memories.

"But it wasn't their decision. It was ours. And they all came around when they understood that it was about our happiness, not theirs." She paused and pushed out a breath. "Alan is like a brother to you. He's your best friend *and* your business partner. You can't let your personal feelings about his choices interfere with that. You *will* wind up the loser."

He stared into her eyes. He knew she was right and he was being obstinate.

"I guess what bothers me more than anything is that he didn't confide in me."

"That's what's really ticking you off. Alan went and did something without you knowing."

"We talk about everything, ya know. I was blind-sided when I walked in that door."

"I'm sure he had his reasons. And I'm sure he would have told you when the time was right for him."

"Yeah," he grumbled. "So what are you saying exactly?" He had the makings of a smile on his face.

"I'm saying you need to go over there and apologize and you need to stop threatening people." She feigned a frown while wagging a finger at him.

"I hate it when you're right."

"I know." She laughed lightly. "Besides you know you're only half the brains of the operation and I'm sick of you walking around here like a caged bear. Go over there and apologize. Matter of fact, invite them both over here. I'll cook."

He slowly shook his head, but his expression was light. "I so hate it when you're right," he repeated.

"Somebody's gotta be." She walked away. "Call him," she said over her shoulder.

Dominique was in Alan's small office researching treatment centers in the Atlanta area. What she hoped to accomplish through therapy was to get at the core of why she turned to alcohol at the first signs of trouble—and not just one drink but bingeing. It was frightening. It wasn't that she needed a drink every day but it seemed to be the only thing that she could grab on to when she felt herself falling.

"Hey, whatcha doing?" Alan asked peeking into the study.

"Checking out some rehab places here in Atlanta." She pushed back a little from the desk.

Alan came in and sat down on the edge of the desk. "Any luck?"

"There are a few. Nothing that really stands out."

He crossed his wrists over his thighs. "I was thinking…and looking into a few things myself. I was thinking that maybe you might be better served seeing someone privately. Ya know, like a psychologist."

She blinked several times. "A psychologist?"

"Yeah, I mean I just don't think that you need to check in anywhere. Talk to someone, get their take on it and move from there." He studied her face. "What do you think?"

She shrugged slightly. "It would be a lot more private," she said thoughtfully.

"Exactly."

"Do you know someone…personally?"

"Actually, I do. I went to see her a few times myself when I was trying to figure out how to deal with Adrienne. I'd started thinking that her erratic behavior was somehow my fault." He blew out a breath. "She'd recommended repeatedly that Adrienne come in to see her or *someone,* but Adrienne refused and I didn't push it like I should have." Regret and guilt tugged down the corners of his mouth.

Dominique placed a gentle hand on his knee. "You couldn't have known."

He got up and moved away. "That's what I keep telling myself." He clenched his jaw. "Easier said than done."

"Maybe you should go and talk to her as well, get stuff off your chest. We could do it together or something."

He gave her a half grin. "Oh, like a package deal."

"Yeah, buy two you get egg rolls for free." She giggled.

The ringing phone intruded. Alan reached for the phone on the desk.

"Hello?" His eyes widened. His expression softened. "Sure. When? I'll let her know. See you then." He hung up the phone and looked at Dominique. "That was Brian. He and Stacy want us to come over for dinner tomorrow night. They want to get to know you."

Her heart thumped. "Tomorrow?"

"Yep."

She drew in a breath. "Well, we have our day cut out for us. Lunch with my sister and dinner with your brother- and sister-in-law."

"Whatever shall we wear?" he mocked in a very bad British accent.

Dominique giggled, jumped up and wrapped her arms around his neck. She looked deeply into his eyes. "I do love you."

He brushed her hair away from her face. "I could really get used to hearing you say that." His mouth claimed hers and when it did he felt certain that nothing in his life had ever felt so right.

The following morning, as Dominique and Alan were preparing for the day ahead, Dominique got a call on her cell phone from Manny.

"How are things, Dominique?" Manny asked.

"Things are finally making sense," she said, walking around the bedroom she shared with Alan. She told him about her talk with her sister and their impending lunch.

"That is making progress. I'm happy for you."

"There's something else that you should know."

"What?"

"I'm staying with Alan Conners."

Dead silence.

"Manny?"

He cleared his throat. "I won't even ask how that happened. That's not important. What is important is that until your divorce is final you need to break it off."

"What?"

"Dominique, you have no idea of the ramifications. If Clif were to get wind of this, he'd have a field day, not to mention the press. I'm sure that Clif would use it against you, say that you were the one who cheated and that's why he had the affair. Or worse, the press will concoct a story that you were somehow behind Alan's wife's suicide."

"I don't care what Clif thinks! I give less than a damn what the press thinks. They've already crucified me."

"What about your future, your career? You can come back from bad movies, but recovering from a personal scandal is a different story."

She hesitated a moment. "That's not important."

"You say that now, in the heat of passion, in the heat of the moment, but what about next month, next year? Men are always forgiven for their indiscretions, but not women. It's a sad double standard but it's true."

"I love him, Manny. I'm not going to give him up."

"I didn't say give him up. I'm saying that you need to put this relationship on the back burner until everything is settled. I'm sure Percy would tell you the exact same thing."

She heard the water in the shower stop. Alan would be coming out any minute.

"I'll think about it, Manny."

"Don't think...*do*."

"I've got to go. Thanks for calling. Thanks for everything." She disconnected the call just as the bathroom door opened.

Alan walked out, wiping is face and hair with a towel. "Deciding on what to wear to the first shindig of the day?" he quipped, draping the towel around his neck.

"Um, I was looking."

His brows drew together. "Are you okay? You look a little stressed. You aren't worried about lunch are you?"

She put on a smile. "Just a little nervous, that's all." She strolled over to him. "It'll be fine."

He pulled her close. "That it will. And when today is over we can come home and celebrate."

"Celebrate?"

"Yeah, this is meet-the-in-laws day. We survive, we celebrate." He winked.

Dominique laughed. "Since you put it that way." She kissed him lightly on the lips and eased out of his hold. "I better get ready."

Dominique went into the bathroom and shut the door. She glanced across the room and her reflection in the mirror stared back at her. She drew in a shaky breath. Was Manny right? Was she on another road to disaster? If she ruined any chance she might have to resuscitate her career, what would she do with the rest of her life? Yes, Alan had asked her to marry him but things change, people change. She'd been on the receiving end of that already.

She walked over to the shower stall and turned on the jets. Without her career she was nothing. Just another has-been pretty face. She was sure that Alan would find a project of his to put her in if she wanted, but she didn't want the world to view her as a charity case—that the only one willing to work with her was her own husband.

She tilted her head upward and closed her eyes. Maybe she should listen to Manny. In all the years they'd worked together he'd never steered her wrong. She'd left her life in the hands of others most of her life. Now it was time for her to plan for her own future.

## Chapter 25

"Your sister is really nice," Alan said as they entered his house.

"She likes you. I can tell. And Brian and Stacy are both wonderful. I can see why you two have been friends for so long."

He put his arm around her waist as they climbed the stairs. "We survived!" he said, kissing her on the cheek.

"What were you and Brian all huddled up about?"

"I want to talk to you about that."

He opened the door to the bedroom, stepped out of his shoes and put them in the closet then turned to her.

"What is it?"

"I need to go back to New York for a few days. The financiers want to meet with us again."

"Oh. When are you leaving?"

"Day after tomorrow."

Her brows shot upward. "Day after tomorrow?"

"I know its last minute, but that's how these things work. You know that."

She sat down on the edge of the bed. "Hey, if you gotta go, you gotta go."

"I'll be back before you know it. And when I return we can go and see Dr. Phillips. She's great and I know you'll like her."

She nodded. "So how long is a few days?"

"Three, four tops. I promise." He came over to her and sat down. "I don't want to be away from you that long and if it wouldn't cause another media storm, I would take you with me."

"I know." She clasped his hand. "I'll be fine."

He kissed the tip of her nose. "I know."

They made sweet slow love that night, reaffirming their feelings and commitment in both words and actions. And as Dominique lay nestled against Alan, listening to his steady breathing, she knew that it would be the last time they'd be together for a while, maybe for good.

"I'll call you as soon as we land at JFK," Alan said. He kissed her once, twice, then snaked his tongue into her mouth, just to hear her moan. She clung to him and he was two seconds from telling the world to go to hell so that he could spend eternity with Dominique.

Brian's car horn blared again.

Reluctantly, Alan eased away from her hot mouth. "I love you," he said, brushing her mouth once more.

"I love you, too." She pressed her head against his chest, closed her eyes to memorize the sound of his heart.

The car horn blasted again.

"Damn, he's gonna get me thrown out of the neighborhood." He gave Dominique a long look. "Talk to you in a few hours. Promise."

She nodded as he backed his way to the door then swiftly turned and jogged down the three steps to the car.

Dominique stood in the doorway and waved as they drove off. She closed the door behind her and drew in a long breath of resolve. She hurried upstairs to find a number for a car service.

Four hours later, Dominique stared out of the airplane window. In another six hours she would be back in L.A., back in the lion's den. She leaned against the headrest and ignored the in-flight movie. She owed Manny big time for this. When she'd called him and told him that she'd thought about what he'd said and wanted to come back, he booked her on the very next flight.

She folded her arms across her stomach. She should have told Alan. But she felt sure that Alan would either try to talk her out of it or insist that he go with her. She needed to do this alone. She needed to *be* alone.

Dominique reached under the seat in front of her, pulled out her tote bag and took out her journal. She flipped it open to a fresh page and saw that there were only a few clean sheets left. She would have to add some new ones soon.

In her perfect small script she poured out her feelings about Alan and how his being in her life had made her believe in happiness again. She wrote about her sister and meeting Brian and Stacy. She wrote about her doubts about leaving Alan without saying anything and how she would make it up to him. But in order to do that she needed to put her past behind her once and for all so that she could freely move into the future. She hoped that Alan would be there.

Manny met her at the airport.

"You look great," he said, not hiding his pleasure. "Life out of the spotlight seems to have worked for you."

"That and being in love with a wonderful man," she said turning to look at him from the passenger seat.

"I'm glad you made this decision, Dominique," he replied, sidestepping her comment about Alan. "If you ever hope to resuscitate your career this is a good move. Your interviews are scheduled for tomorrow morning and I've set up a meeting with a treatment counselor for six this evening. After hours." He gave her a pointed look.

Dominique drew in a breath and nodded. "Thanks." She glanced out the window as the California landscape whizzed by.

"You'll stay at my house."

"Thanks," she murmured, thinking of Alan and missing him already. He would be worried when he couldn't reach her.

After the short drive from the airport, they arrived at Manny's home. Evelyn was there to greet them.

She opened her arms in welcome. "Good to see you," she said against Dominique's ear.

"Thanks for letting me hang out here."

"Anytime. Come on in and make yourself comfortable. Hungry? I know airline food is practically nonexistent," she said with a chuckle.

"I am a little hungry."

"Great. I'll whip us up something. Your same room is prepared for you. Go get settled and come down when you're ready."

Manny came in behind them carrying Dominique's bag. "I'll go up with your bag." He followed Dominique upstairs and put her bag in her room. "It's good to have you back." He held her at arm's length. "We're going to make this work."

"I know," she said softly.

"Well, get settled and then come on down. We

need to go over a few things. We can eat and talk."
He walked out.

Dominique strolled over to the bed and put down
her tote bag. The next couple of days would be
grueling. That much she was certain of. She was
prepared. It was time for her to stand on her own, face
the music and dance.

She sat down on the side of the bed and pulled out
her cell phone. There were already two messages
from Alan. She drew in a breath of resolve and
returned his call.

"Hey, babe," he answered. She could hear the
pleasure and relief in his voice. "I called a couple of
times. Hanging out?"

"Actually, I'm in L.A."

There was moment of dead silence.

Finally, Alan spoke. "Did you say L.A.?"

Dominique swallowed. "Yes. I left shortly after
you did."

"Color me slow but I don't get it. What are you
doing in L.A. and why didn't you say something?"

"I need to take care of some things."

"And you couldn't tell me?"

"Manny wants me to do some interviews."

"It's still not making sense, Dominique. What was
so secret that you couldn't tell me that you were
going halfway across the damned country?"

She shut her eyes. "We need to spend some time
apart for a little while." She gripped the phone. "Until

my divorce is finalized I can't risk anyone finding out about us. There's no telling what Clifton would do with that kind of information."

"And the answer is to walk out on me without a word. Is that what you're telling me?"

"Alan, I knew if I told you you'd find a way to convince me to stay and I would have weakened and done it."

"Nikki, we're supposed to be a team. Teams talk about stuff and do stuff together, they make decisions together." His voice hardened with each word. "At least, that's what I always thought. You've obviously proved me wrong."

Her chest constricted. "I need to do this, Alan. If I don't have my career, I don't have anything. I'm not going to spend the rest of my life being dependent on anyone. I can't do it and that's exactly what would happen if I can't repair what's left of my career."

"Fine." He snorted nastily. "Do what you have to do, Dominique. Hmph, guess I'll see you…on television." He disconnected the call.

Dominique bit down on her bottom lip to keep from crying. It had to be done. She returned her phone to her purse and went to join her hosts.

# Chapter 26

"What is bugging you?" Brian asked as they got into the Town car en route to their meeting. "You've been acting like your shorts are too tight all morning."

"Forget it."

"I would if I knew what I was supposed to be forgetting. What gives?"

Alan gritted his teeth.

"You're gonna crack your damned jaw if you don't chill."

Alan released a long breath of disappointment and frustration and shook his head. "I guess I may as well tell you before you see it on television."

"Television! What the he—"

Alan held up his hand. "It's nothing to do with us. It's Dominique."

Brian's puffed up chest slowly deflated. "Not another…incident?"

"No, nothing like that."

"Then what?"

"She went back to L.A."

Brian frowned in confusion. "What are you talking about? When?"

"Apparently she left shortly after we did."

"And I take it you knew nothing about it."

"Right."

Brian made several bemused motions with his hands. "So, I'm still not getting it. Why is she there and why didn't she tell you?"

"I have no clue. All she would say is that she had things to take care of and if she'd told me she felt I would have tried to stop her."

Brian was silent for a moment trying to make sense of it all. "Hey man, I wish I knew what to tell you." He shrugged helplessly. He looked at Alan. "You mentioned television. You wanna tell me what you mean by that?"

"She said she had some interviews to do on a couple of the morning shows."

"Hey man, listen. Maybe she should have told you. She didn't. It ain't the end of the world. I'm sure she has a good explanation. It's probably all about her career—damage control or something." He slapped Alan on the thigh. "It'll be fine. What you need to concentrate on right now are the folks who hold our future in their hands. When we get back, sit down with her and hash it out."

Alan pursed his lips. "Yeah," he muttered. "Nothing I can do about it now."

But that didn't stop Alan from wondering what else Dominique would keep from him if the mood hit her? How many mornings would he wake up and simply find her gone? He tugged on his tie. When he was finished in New York he had every intention of finding out the answers to all of his questions.

On the other side of the country, the sun was only a vague orange glow hovering above the horizon. A gentle morning breeze lifted the light curtain in the window. Dominique stretched beneath the cool cotton sheet. With slow deliberation, she opened her eyes and the moment she did a tense, unsettled feeling gripped hold of her stomach. She drew in a long deep breath to calm the flutters.

She turned her head toward the partially opened bay window. Today was the day. Her first interview since…well, since the Primrose Motel. She was due in the studios of *The Morning Agenda* at six. From experience she knew that much of that time would be taken up sitting around and waiting. Manny had jockeyed for the seven o'clock segment—the segment with the most viewers, the segment just before everyone rushed out to work.

From there she was scheduled to go on *The View* and *The Ellen DeGeneres Show*. Manny hadn't left any stone unturned for the media-blitz comeback. She would have every forum available to tell her story the way she wanted it to be told.

Dominique sat up in bed, pushed the covers down to her knees. In the distance she could hear movement and assumed that Manny was getting ready for the day ahead.

She tossed the covers aside then glanced at her cell phone on the nightstand. By rote she picked it up to check for messages. She knew wishing was futile, but she did hope for a message from Alan. No message, not even so much as an indication of a call from him. She put the phone down. She couldn't blame him. What did she expect after the stunt she pulled? Dominique got out of bed and went to take her shower.

"You look great," Manny said when Dominique joined him and Evelyn in the kitchen.

Evelyn yawned loudly. "Coffee is ready," she mumbled.

Manny chuckled. "Evelyn is not a morning person."

"Have a good show or whatever it is they say." She patted Dominique's arm and shuffled back to bed.

Manny turned to Dominique. "Ready?"

"As ready as I can be." She went to the side

counter and filled her mug with coffee and added some Sweet'n Low and cream. "I'll just be glad when it's all over." She looked into Manny's eyes. "Do you think it will be worth it?"

"Worth what? Standing up for yourself? Telling your side of the story? Stamping out rumors and gaining back your dignity?" He nodded somberly. "Yes, I think it will be worth it."

"Even if it means ruining the best thing that's ever happened to me in the process?"

Manny took two steps toward her. "If there is one thing I've learned in this business and in life, if someone is meant to be in your life, bumps in the road won't take them off course. If he cares for you as much as you care for him, he'll get over his wounded ego and he'll understand that you needed to do this for you."

She looked at him and smiled weakly. "All right, Mr. DeMille, I'm ready for my close-up."

He put his arm around her shoulder. "That's my girl."


"Welcome back to The Morning Agenda. I'm Faith Lloyd and as promised I'm here with Dominique Laws." She turned her hundred-watt smile on Dominique. "Thank you for coming, Dominique."

"Good to be here."

"There has been so much controversy swirling around you since your loss at the Golden Globes—

the pictures taken of you at the motel and the stunning announcement by your former housekeeper. Some say your career is over."

Dominique lifted her chin ever so slightly. A calm settled over her the way it always did when a director shouted *action*. "I also heard a rumor that I was dead, but that isn't true, either."

Faith laughed lightly.

"What is true is that for the first time in my life I ran smack into a brick wall and instead of going around it I kept running right into it. I'd grown so accustomed to having everyone take care of my every concern that I simply didn't know what to do for myself and I turned to drinking."

"Are you getting help or do you feel you need to?"

"Yes, which is another reason why I came back to the coast. I felt the best way to deal with my demons was to face them."

Faith put on her best compassionate expression. "I know this must be very hard to talk about…but your husband, Clif Burrell—he's been not only your husband but also your business manager for years. What were you feeling when you heard about your husband and your housekeeper?"

For a hot second she wanted to tell her what an asinine question that was, but knew better.

"I felt the same way any wife would have felt… stunned, angry, betrayed, humiliated. I felt it all and for a time I let it get the best of me. But with the love and support of family and friends I'm dealing with all of it."

"Have you spoken to your housekeeper since she made her very public announcement?"

"No, and I don't intend to."

"The day that you were photographed at the motel," she said, looking and sounding very solemn and sincere. "What was going through your mind?"

"I think I'd hit rock bottom. My career was falling apart, my husband was having an affair, I felt alone and confused. It was a difficult time for me."

"Do you plan to work again?"

"I don't think there is anyone in this business who has not had their personal trials come under scrutiny." She drew in a breath and slowly exhaled. "There's an old saying that goes something like…what doesn't kill you makes you stronger. I've had a lot to deal with these past few months. It bent me but it didn't break me. As any actor will tell you, channeling your own experiences enriches your roles." She laughed lightly. "And I have plenty of experiences to channel."

Faith leaned forward. "Dominique, thank you so much for getting up so early and talking with us. As a fan of your work, I know I'll be looking forward to seeing you back on the big screen."

"Thank you, Faith."

Faith turned to the camera. "Next up, Stan Ingram with your local weather."

When the camera light went off, Faith stuck out

her hand, which Dominique shook. "Thank you so much. I really am a fan. That wasn't a line I was handing you."

"I appreciate that, Faith."

"Best of luck."

"Thank you."

A technician came and disconnected Dominique's microphone. Manny was there to meet her as she returned backstage.

"You okay?" he asked gently.

"Actually, I feel pretty good."

"Great. You're a born star." He kissed the top of her head. "We've got to hustle to our next stop. Oh, and I was able to wrangle a dinner interview with the editor from *Variety*. An exclusive."

"You've definitely earned your fifteen percent."

"You should also arrange to see Percy while you're out here."

"I intend to. I'll give him a call in the car."

The rest of the day's interviews went well even if they were a little taxing. Dominique answered all the intimate questions as honestly as she could. What she wanted to get across more than anything was that she was not a helpless victim who would be humiliated into obscurity. Yes, she was a public figure and her life was under more scrutiny that most, but that did not justify the crucifixion she'd received in the media over the past few months. Her personal life was painful enough to have to deal with without it being a news event.

"How are you holding up?" Manny asked.

"Exhausted but okay. I needed to do this," she said thoughtfully. "As long as I stayed in the shadows hiding out, it was open season for the media to come up with whatever angle they wanted. At least now they've heard my side."

"And it's important for the studios, producers, the whole lot of them to know that you're still in the game and taking control of your life."

She nodded. "Exactly."

"What time are we meeting Percy?"

"He said he'd meet us at the restaurant at eight."

"Good. That will give us plenty of time to freshen up and unwind for a little bit."

She sat back in the car. The television stuff was over. Tomorrow was her sit-down interview with *Variety*. She wondered if Alan had seen any of the television shows and if he did how was he feeling about it. She'd desperately wanted to tell the world that he was the source of her newfound strength, but knew that it would be disastrous to both of them. If only they could both hold out until the time was right and this storm was behind her, she knew they would be all right.

Alan aimed the remote at the television and shut it off. Dominique had been poised, beautiful and brutally honest about everything she'd gone through. It was clear that she had no intention of succumbing to the scandals, the betrayals or the rumors.

As much as he was reluctant to admit it, she was right about not telling him. He would have wanted to be with her and that's not what she needed or wanted. She had to find a way to break free of all the restraints and expectations, do this her way and on her own.

He leaned back. Patience wasn't one of his virtues but he realized that he was going to have to master it if he had any intention of keeping Dominique in his life. This was all going to take time. But anything worth having is worth waiting for.

*Chapter 27*

Percy stood up when Dominique approached, escorted to the table by the hostess. Several heads turned in recognition as she wound her way around the tables. She looked every bit the star in a cool cream silk top and matching pants. She'd pulled her thick shoulder-length hair back into a soft knot at the nape of her neck. Tiny diamond studs sparkled from her ears. Her caramel complexion was free of makeup, except for mascara, which accentuated her long lashes and large doe-shaped eyes, and a bronze gloss that made her full lips shimmer. Dominique kept her pleasant expression in place and her eyes ahead. She looked healthy and rested, Percy thought as she drew closer. And she appeared to have lost a few pounds, which suited her height. He was surprised, however, that Manny wasn't with her.

"Great to see you again, Dominique," Percy said. He helped her into her seat. "I thought Manny would be with you."

She explained that she had insisted, after a lengthy debate, that she didn't need Manny to accompany her. Finally, he gave in, realizing that she wouldn't be moved. He'd given her the keys to his car and sent her on her way.

Percy chuckled, knowing how possessive Manny was of Dominique and knowing that Dominique must have put up a damned good fight. "Good for you. So...how does it feel being back on this side of the world?"

"Not as scary as I'd thought," she said with a hint of laughter in her voice. She took a surreptitious glance around from beneath her long lashes.

The waitress approached. "Would you like to order now?"

"I'll have a martini on the rocks," Percy said. He looked to Dominique.

"Sparkling water with a twist of lemon, please."

"I'll be right back to take your food orders."

Dominique put her purse on top of the table. "So where are we with everything?"

"No chatting about the weather first with you," he joked. He folded his hands on top of the table. "All of your paperwork has been filed. Still no sign or word from Clifton. That could be good or bad."

Her heart knocked in her chest. "What do you mean, *good or bad?*"

"Well, every now and again you'll get a judge that wants you to exhaust every possible avenue to locate the other party, especially when there is money and property involved. I'm hoping that when we get a court date, which should be soon, we'll have a judge that wants to see you out of this mess as much as you do."

"But Clifton took all the money. The houses are in his name."

"True, but this is California, remember."

"I don't want anything. Nothing. I just want to end this marriage and move on with my life."

"That's what we'll work toward." He cleared his throat. "When this is all over, have you thought about what you're going to do for money? I mean, I know nine thousand dollars can't be lasting very much longer. Any potential movie roles, television?"

"Hopefully after the media blitz that Manny pulled together I'll get some offers coming in. But for now I want to take my time and not jump on the first thing that comes along."

"Understandable."

The waitress returned with their drinks and took their dinner order.

"How long do you plan to stay out here?" Percy asked.

She looked directly at him. "As long as it takes."

* * *

Clifton answered the door. It was room service. He'd grown quite used to hotel life and being in Las Vegas wasn't half bad, either. Everyone was a tourist and every face was innocuous. No one knew him from Adam.

The waiter wheeled the cart into the center of the suite and lifted the silver covers to display his order.

Clifton reached into his robe pocket—courtesy of the hotel—and tipped the waiter a handsome ten dollars and was thanked profusely.

He pushed the cart in front of the couch and turned on the television. The last face he expected to see was Dominique's. She was on *Ellen*. He turned up the volume and hung on to every word.

*She looks wonderful* was his first reaction and it hit him like a falling anvil how much he missed her. The realization was so sudden and unexpected it took the wind out of him.

He listened as she talked candidly about her ordeal, not only her bouts of drinking but how the dissolution of her marriage had affected her.

"When I got married I thought it would be forever. I was very much in love with my husband." She looked sad for a moment but quickly recovered. "No one can prepare you for betrayal and nothing can prepare you for having every detail of your personal life broadcasted, dissected and discussed around the world. It makes a difficult situation that much more difficult. But I'm handling it."

"Did you have any idea that your husband was seeing someone else?"

"No. I didn't. Maybe there were signs and I missed them. I don't know. But things happen in a marriage over time. My only regret is that we weren't able to talk about it between us before it got blown up out of proportion. What happened between my husband and me happens in households every day. The difference is that I'm a known commodity."

"It's a high price to pay for fame."

"It certainly is."

"With that in mind do you have any regrets?"

"No. I don't hold anyone but myself at fault. No one can do anything to you that you don't allow them to do. For a long time everyone but me ran my life. That's the only thing that I intend to change."

"What are your plans for the future?" Ellen asked.

Dominique offered a soft smile. "I'll be starting counseling and I hope it will help me to understand myself better and how better to cope with life's pitfalls without having to turn to a crutch."

"Do you think you'll ever get married again?"

"I'm a romantic at heart. I love the idea of being a couple, part of a team. But before I even consider anything permanent with anyone, I want to be sure that I'm strong inside and out. I'm taking everything one day at a time."

"Any movie roles on the horizon?"

Dominique laughed. "Let's just say that no one is

beating down my door at the moment, but I'm hopeful. Outside of everything that has happened in the past few months, I'm still an actress. I love what I do and I think I'm good at it. Hopefully, a director out there is thinking of me for their next big movie. And if not," she shrugged slightly, "I'll deal with it."

"I'm sure your fans will flock to the theaters to see you again. *Misdemeanors* is still my favorite film."

"Thank you."

"Stay where you are," Ellen said into the camera. "We'll be right back with Justin Timberlake."

Clifton stared at the screen until the picture dissolved to the commercial.

That was not the Dominique he knew. This Dominique was confident, not because words were put into her mouth but because she'd changed. All the years they were together he'd been in control—from what she wore to what she said to where she went to what roles she played. He thrived on her dependency. The weaker she was the stronger he felt. He never gave her an opportunity to be anything other than the person he'd created. And then not even that was enough. He lost his grip and she soared out of his reach. It wasn't Dominique that was nothing without him. He was nothing without her. She had stepped back out in the world and he was the one in hiding. If it weren't so sad it would almost be funny.

He stared at his steak, salad and baked potato. Suddenly he wasn't hungry. He'd made a terrible mistake and lost the only person that mattered because of his stupid ego. He'd known as much for months but had been too stubborn to admit it. Somewhere in the back of his mind he hoped that Dominique would come to him, realize that she needed him. She didn't.

He pushed the cart aside. If Dominique could stand up under the blinding lights and look at them head on, so could he. There was so much he needed to fix. All he could hope for was that it wasn't too late. And if Marcia's allegation that the child she carried was his was found to be true, he'd have to stand up to his responsibilities and take care of his child and Marcia.

Clifton walked into the master bedroom and went to the phone. He booked the next flight to Los Angeles.

Dominique was preparing for bed when an image flashed on the television screen. Her heart stood still. She turned up the volume as the newscaster spoke.

"Clifton Burrell, estranged husband to actress Dominique Laws was involved in a car accident en route to the Nevada airport. Our on-site reporter has up-to-the-minute details."

"Yes, Chris, it's a horrific scene here. Fire trucks and EMS workers are lining the highway in the five-car pileup. According to police, there are already two fatalities. Apparently an SUV lost control and swerved into oncoming traffic. One car went over the dividing rail. Helicopters were brought in to airlift survivors from this firey crash to area hospitals."

"We have word that Clifton Burrell was one of the victims. Is that correct?"

"Yes it is, Chris. He was flown to Los Angeles Medical Center. No word on his condition. He had to be cut out of the wreckage. His driver is one of the fatalities."

"That was Thomas Chase at the scene on Nevada's highway 95. We'll keep viewers posted as more details become available. In other news…"

For several moments, Dominique stood frozen in front of the set, trying to absorb what she'd just heard. She looked up and Manny and Evelyn were standing in her bedroom doorway.

"We just saw the news," Evelyn said.

Evelyn's voice snapped her out of her trance. She blinked several times and tried to find her voice.

"What do you want to do?" Manny asked gently.

All the years with Clifton flashed before her, the good and the bad. "I…I need to go to the hospital."

"Of course. We'll drive you," Evelyn offered.

When she looked again, Manny was standing in front of her, wiping her eyes with his handkerchief. She hadn't even realized that she was crying. She sniffed and took gulping breaths.

"Sit down for a minute," Manny said, ushering her toward the bed.

She waved him off. "No. We need to go." She looked imploringly from one to the other.

"Of course."

Dominique grabbed her purse and jacket.

By the time they arrived at the hospital, television cameras and reporters had already staked out the hospital entrance. Fortunately, they were kept on the opposite side of the street by the police. The instant she stepped out of the car the media erupted in a frenzy of shouting and camera flashes. Even though she had a baseball cap pulled low over her head and was dressed like a soccer mom on her way to the supermarket, she couldn't hide from the discerning eye of the media.

"Will you take your husband back if he makes it?" a reporter shouted.

"Has the mother of his child been notified? Have you spoken to her?"

Manny put his arm protectively around her shoulders and hustled her inside with Evelyn bringing up the rear. They went straight to the emergency desk.

"I'm Dominique Laws. My…husband Clifton Burrell…"

The nurse's eyes widened. "Ms. Laws. Your husband is being worked on in the trauma room."

"Can I see him?"

"I'm sorry. Not until they can stabilize. He went into cardiac arrest when he was brought in."

Dominique's hand went to her mouth to stifle a gasp.

"You can wait in the lounge. I'm sure the doctors will let you see him as soon as possible. I'll let them know that you're here."

Dominique nodded and blindly walked to the waiting room. Manny and Evelyn took seats on either side of her. They sat in silence holding hands for what seemed to be an eternity.

It was more than an hour later when the doctor entered the waiting room. Dominique jumped to her feet. Her heart raced when she saw the grave look on the doctor's face.

"Ms. Laws?"

"Yes!" She held her breath.

"Your husband has sustained severe internal injuries. We've stabilized him enough to get him to the operating room. He's already gone into arrest once. There's a very strong chance that he may not make it or because of the extensive blood loss that he could slip into a coma. We need to know what you want to do regarding resuscitation."

"W-what? I don't understand."

"In the event that things take a turn for the worse, we need to know what your wishes are—as next of kin—regarding means of keeping him alive."

Dominique's knees wobbled. Manny grabbed her around the waist to keep her on her feet. She slumped against him. Evelyn rushed over with a cup of water.

"We need a decision, Ms. Laws."

"Do whatever you must to keep him…alive."

The doctor nodded and started to hurry off.

"Can I see him? Please."

The doctor stopped, and turned to Dominique. "Follow me."

Dominique hurried behind the doctor to the trauma room. The nurses and orderlies were busy preparing Clifton for surgery.

"Only a minute."

Dominique swallowed over the dry knot in her throat. She walked up to the gurney and when she looked down at Clifton her stomach lurched up to her throat.

If the doctors hadn't told her this was her husband she wouldn't have recognized him. His face was a mass of gashes and bruises, his eyes were almost swollen shut and his mouth was three times its normal size.

She took his hand. It was icy cold. "Clif. It's Dom."

He groaned and tried to open the slits that were now his eyes. She bent closer to hear his whisper.

"I'm…sorry…for everything. I was on my way to L.A. to…tell you." He suddenly gripped her hand. "I shouldn't have…hurt you." His tears slid down to the pillow. "Please forgive…"

The monitors attached to his body began a frantic bleating. A doctor rushed to the gurney, pushing Dominique aside. "He's crashing!"

The medical team grabbed the gurney and raced down the hallway, leaving Dominique to watch the ominous departure. Quiet sobs shook her body. She pressed her fist to her mouth as the scene in front of her blurred from her tears.

"Dom, come on, honey." It was Evelyn. She put her arm around Dominique and walked her back to the waiting room.

Less than a half hour later, the doctor returned. The look on his face said it all.

Dominique gasped yet still hoped. The doctor approached.

"I'm sorry. We lost him. We did everything we could but his injuries were too severe. The blood loss…" He paused a beat, looked at each shocked face. "I'm sorry." He turned and walked away.

Dominique slumped back against the hard plastic seat and covered her face with her hands. She heard Manny saying something to Evelyn about making arrangements, but she couldn't even react. It was like a bad dream. Sure, she wanted Clifton out of her life, but not like this, never like this. *I'm sorry.* She heard Clif's voice float to her consciousness.

"Dominique, come on, honey, let's get you home."

The next thing that she remembered was waking up the following morning in the guest bedroom of Manny and Evelyn's house. The sun streamed through the window. It was a beautiful day. She sat up slowly, sensing that something was wrong. Then reality hit her, sucking the air from her lungs. Clifton was gone. The thought bounced around and around in her head. That sick feeling in the pit of her stomach was back. She shut her eyes against her last images of Clif just as her cell phone rang.

Wearily, she looked at the silver object shimmying across the nightstand. She reached for it and her heart thundered in her chest when she saw the number on the lighted dial.

"Alan," she breathed in happiness and trepidation.

"Baby, I heard. I'm so sorry. I wanted to call earlier. What can I do?"

"Just hearing your voice…" Her eyes filled with water.

"I can be there late this evening."

"Alan, there's so much going on. I…" Her mind tumbled over the myriad of things to be taken care of, not the least of which was dealing with the press.

"Look, I'm not taking no for an answer. I'll stay in a hotel. I'll meet you in a dark alley if need be. But I'm not going to let you go through this by yourself. The hell with the press and what they think they know."

She almost smiled. "Come," she whispered. "I need you."

"That's all I needed to hear. I'll be on the next flight and I'll call you the minute I land."

"Okay." She was shaky all over. "There's so much that we need to talk about, things I need to tell you."

"They can wait—"

"No, they can't. If I've learned nothing else out of this tragedy with Clif it's that nothing is promised. You can't wait for tomorrow or later to say what's on your mind and heart or to fix the things that need to be fixed." She swallowed and took a breath. "I love you, Alan. Love you with all my heart and soul. I want to be with you. I'm sorry for leaving you the way I did and the thought that I might not be able to make it up to you was killing me inside. I'm ready to have a life with you, whatever that may be."

Alan was so overwhelmed by the passion and sincerity of Dominique's declaration that he was momentarily speechless.

"Alan?"

He cleared his throat. "Yes, I'm here. I needed to hear that."

"I needed to say it."

"Is there anything I can do for you before I see you?"

"Just get here as soon as you can."

"I love you, Nikki. I'll see you soon."

Dominique held the phone to her chest. She knew the next few days were going to be an ordeal, but with Alan at her side she would be ready.

She got up from bed, pulled herself together and went downstairs. Manny was on the phone in the kitchen. Evelyn was making coffee.

"How did you sleep?" Evelyn asked.

"I think I was more knocked out than asleep," she admitted. "As soon as Manny is done I wanted to talk to both of you." She took a seat at the island counter. Evelyn handed her a mug of coffee.

Manny wrapped up his call and joined them. "That was the editor from *Variety*. Obviously, we're not doing the interview." He looked at Dominique. "How are you doing this morning?"

"Still in shock, but okay." She drew in a breath then looked from one to the other. "I wanted you both to know that Alan is coming. I just got off the phone with him. He's catching the next flight." She swallowed, waiting for a reaction.

"Are you sure him being here is the best thing?" Manny asked, surprising her with his calm.

"It's what I want, what we want. We'll deal with the media if we choose to. What more can they possibly do to me?"

Manny reached over and patted her hand. "As your agent, I'd say don't do it." He glanced at his wife then at Dominique. "But as your friend, I say follow your heart."

Dominique gave a tight smile of thanks. "I better get dressed. We have a long day."

The trio spent the better part of the day making arrangements for Clifton. They planned a private ceremony and private burial. None of the information was to be disclosed to the media. By the time they arrived back at Manny's house they were mentally and physically exhausted.

"I'm going to order Chinese," Evelyn announced.

"Fine by me," Manny agreed, running his fingers through his hair.

"I'm going to run up and change then head to the

airport." Alan had text-messaged her earlier to say that his plane would be landing at LAX at 9:00 p.m. "Would it be okay if I used the car?"

"Of course," Manny said. "I'd be happy to drive you," he said and followed his offer with a wide yawn.

"You've done more than enough. Thanks." She went upstairs. As she took a quick shower and got dressed while intermittently keeping her eye on the clock. She realized, even with things as they were, she couldn't deny the feeling of bubbling anticipation at seeing Alan.

As she walked through the airport to the passenger pickup she didn't see all of the bustling passengers, airport personnel or hear the countless announcements over the loud speakers. The only thing in her mind's eye was Alan's face and the sound of his voice whispering in her ear.

She walked as far as she could before being stopped by security. She peeked over heads and in between bodies as the passengers from Alan's plane began coming out of the gate. Her heart was pounding so hard she could barely breathe. And then she saw him come through the gangway. Her breath caught in her chest and an overwhelming sensation of joy filled her. Nothing else in the world mattered at that moment except getting into his arms and feeling his mouth against hers.

Alan looked out into the waiting crowd and spotted her. For a moment he stood still, needing that instant to take her in. A slow smile moved across his mouth and lighted a fire in his eyes. He picked up his pace, nearly knocking a couple over in the process. He muttered his apologies and kept going until he was right on top of her.

Time and space stood still. He dropped his bag at his feet, snaked his hand behind her head and pulled her fully into the kiss he'd been dreaming about since she'd left.

Dominique rose up on her toes to wrap her arms around his neck. His fingers trailed down her back. She moaned against his lips.

"I missed you so much," he said, kissing her.

"So did I." She gazed up into his eyes, stroked his cheeks.

He grinned and looked around. "I think we might be causing a scene."

"You know what…I don't care," she said, her voice light and carefree. "Let them look. I'm in love with Alan Conners and I don't care who knows it!" she shouted, causing looks, some applause and happy smiles. She pulled her baseball cap off her head and waved it in the air.

Alan tossed his head back and laughed. "Come on, woman, before you cause a riot."

Dominique giggled and let Alan usher her to the exit.

Once inside the car they were like two teens that couldn't keep their hands off each other.

"I want you so bad," Alan breathed hotly against her neck. His palm covered her right breast.

Air hissed between her teeth. She ran her hand over the hard bulge in his pants. "If I thought we could do it right here…I would." Her chest heaved with longing.

Alan kissed her hungrily then with great reluctance eased back. "Stay with me tonight." He looked deep into her eyes.

"I thought you'd never ask."

*Chapter 28*

Dominique was on her back, her taut thighs spread to an inviting angle. She cupped her swollen breasts, offering them to Alan who knelt between her legs. He leaned over her and teased one hard nipple, then the other with the tips of his teeth. Dominique whimpered. Her stomach muscles fluttered. Alan reached down between her legs and gently caressed her swollen clit. Her thighs trembled and her pelvis instinctively rose and rocked seductively against his hand.

Alan lowered himself, bracing his weight on his forearms. "I want to spend the rest of my life with you," he said as he slowly eased inside her tight, wet heat. He groaned deep in his throat as she gloved him.

They made slow, deep, passionate love—making up for lost time, reaffirming their commitment, solidifying their feelings.

Alan wanted to be gentle, treat her like delicate porcelain, but the more he tried the more difficult it was for him to contain the fire that roared in his loins. He was so hard and full he felt like he would break. He drove into her and she took him all the way in, asking for more. "Deeper," she whispered. "Faster. Fill me." She cried out as the spasms gripped her like hundreds of volts of electricity.

Dominique clung to him, wrapping her arms and legs tightly around Alan's body, not wanting even air to come between them as he rode them to earth-shattering bliss.

Alan cradled Dominique tightly to his body. He kissed the back of her neck. "Did you decide how long you're going to stay out here on the Coast?"

"As soon as we get everything settled with… Clif…actually, I was considering staying here," she blurted out.

He turned her onto her back and looked into her eyes. "Are you serious?"

She nodded. "I've lived here for the past fifteen years. This is home to me. The business is here. If there is any chance of resurrecting my career, I need to be here."

Alan was quiet for a moment. "Then I want you to stay here at my place."

"Alan, I couldn't—"

"Why not?"

"It's just…for years I lived in 'Clif's house.' I moved out of a home with my sister and into a home with Clif. I've never had to make it on my own." Her brows creased. "Do you understand?"

Alan twisted his mouth to the side. "I don't have to like it do I?"

She laughed lightly.

"But on the real side. How are you going to be able to afford it on your own? You said you were broke."

"I'll figure it out. I'll start out small… I'll rely on the kindness of strangers," she said, in a convincing imitation of Scarlett O'Hara.

Alan chuckled. "You're welcome to stay here anytime you want, whether I'm here or not. I'm going to be back and forth between here and New York for the next few months while we get the production company up and running."

"And I have my own life to get in order."

He cupped her face. "And then when the time is right there won't be any discussion about where we're going to live, 'cause we'll be under one roof as husband and wife."

Her gaze ran over his face. "I love the sound of that."

It had been more than a month since Clifton's passing. Dominique had begun seeing a counselor and was working through her issues of dependency. She was feeling stronger and better about herself and her future. She and Alan spent whatever time they could together, making plans and falling deeper in love. In between, she was working on a project that her counselor had suggested. She was excited and it took all her willpower to keep it a secret from Alan until she was done.

She was returning to her tiny studio apartment from a short trip to the local supermarket. Just as she stepped through the door her phone rang. It was Clifton's attorney.

"Mrs. Burrell, I was hoping that you could come into my office in the morning."

"Why?"

"I think it's best if we talk face-to-face." He gave her his office address and set a time, 10:00 a.m. the following day.

"What do you think he wants?" Alan asked that evening over dinner.

"I don't have a clue."

"Want me to go with you? We're just about wrapped up with the location. I can take some time."

"Sure. That would be great."

"Nikki, how are you fixed for money, seriously?"

She grinned. "Well, the rent is pretty cheap. I still get a check from the video sales of my movies. So for now, I'm okay." She was itching to tell him what she was working on, but knew it wasn't ready yet.

He pursed his lips. "Don't you be too proud to let me know if you need something."

"Alan, you do enough."

He reached across the table. "I want to do it full-time, all of it. You know that."

"I have to take care of myself first. I need to know that I can do it. And I'm getting there day by day."

Dominique and Alan arrived at Lewis Temple's office promptly at ten.

"I'll be right here waiting for you," Alan said, giving her a light kiss on her cheek.

Dominique approached the secretary and was taken into Mr. Temple's office.

"Mrs. Burrell, thank you for coming. Please have a seat." He opened a file folder and spread several sheets of densely typed pages in front of him. He looked up at Dominique and adjusted his bifocals. "Your husband…"

More than a half hour later, Dominique emerged dazed with disbelief. Alan stood the moment she walked out.

"What happened?" he asked, concern lacing his voice from the stunned expression on her face.

Dominique finally focused on Alan. "He… Clif left me everything."

## Chapter 29

Dominique and Alan stood in front of the home she'd lived in with Clifton. The For Sale sign stood prominently on the lawn.

"I still can't believe it," she said. "I didn't even know he had a will."

Alan squeezed her close. "Underneath it all, Clif may have had his faults, but I think deep inside he only wanted the best for you. He just didn't always know how to go about it."

Dominique nodded in agreement. "Well," she breathed, "maybe it's time we went house-hunting."

Alan's head snapped in her direction. She looked at him with a smile like sunshine on her face.

He swept her up in his arms and spun her around in a circle before taking her mouth in a searing kiss. Finally he set her down on her feet amid a flurry of giggles.

"The world is ours, baby," he said, staring deep into her eyes. He dug into the pocket of his jacket and pulled out the box that had been burning a whole in his side for months. He flipped the box open and the diamond snapped, crackled and popped in the sunshine.

Alan got down on one knee right on the lawn and took Dominique's hand in his.

"I love you from the depths of my soul. Both of us have faced our challenges and beat them—individually. I want us to spend the rest of our lives facing the world together. Marry me, Dominique. Let me love you, comfort you, be your best friend, your lover. Be my wife."

Tears tumbled down her cheeks onto their joined hands. Her voice shook so badly she could hardly get the simple word out.

"Yes!"

Alan took the ring from the velvet case and slipped it on her finger then slowly rose to his feet. He held her tenderly against him and kissed her lips.

He held her chin in the palm of his hand. "Your place or mine?" he teased.

"Mine," Dominique said. "There's something that I've been dying to show you."

* * *

Dominique had been sitting out in the small backyard of her building for more than two hours. Every time she heard a sound, she jumped, thinking that it was finally Alan emerging with the verdict. Her heart was pounding out of control. She kept wiping her damp palms on her pant legs.

Finally, the back door opened and Alan stood in the threshold. She tried to swallow but her throat was so dry she knew she'd choke.

Alan took a step toward her, then lowered himself down next to her. She stared into his eyes, hoping to see the answer there.

"It's…brilliant," he said, looking at her in awe.

The rope that was wrapped around her stomach unraveled. She drew in a long breath of relief. Alan set the stack of pages down next to him.

For the past few months she'd been working on turning her journal into a screenplay. She'd never tried her hand at it before, but she'd read enough scripts and she had what she thought was a story worth telling.

"Do you really mean that?"

He nodded. "It left me with so many emotions. It runs the gamut." He took her hand. "But most of all it let me see you…that side of you that the screen has never seen—Dominique the woman, not the actress reading a part, not a character. I want this to be the first film my company produces."

Her heart rose and tumbled in her chest. "And you're not just saying that because you're madly in love with me, are you?" She was grinning like crazy.

"I'm saying that because this is an incredible piece of work that needs to been seen and experienced by the world. I know I can do it justice."

She wrapped her arms around his neck, planted a big wet kiss on his lips, then tossed her head back and let out a joyous whoop.

The sun was beginning to set on the horizon, casting a brilliant orange glow across the water. Dominique and Alan walked hand in hand across the beach, hugging and kissing like the people in love that they were.

"I think a small private ceremony with my sister, Manny and Evelyn, and Brian and Stacy," Dominique said.

"Sounds perfect to me. I was thinking we could honeymoon in Hawaii."

"Hawaii!" She jumped up into his arms and they tumbled onto the sand.

"I think she likes it," he teased.

They shuffled around and sat next to each other, staring out at the water. Dominique rested her head against Alan's shoulder.

A couple walked by and stopped. The girl's eyes widened. "Aren't you that actress…Dominique Laws?" she said, the excitement evident in her voice.

Dominique looked at Alan then up into the questioning eyes of the young woman.

"People mistake me for her all the time," she said with all seriousness.

"Oh, sorry. You look just like her." The couple walked off.

Alan chuckled. "You are a great actress, you know, and you're perfect for playing the main part in your screenplay."

Dominique looked deeply into the eyes of the man she loved. "The only part I want to play from this day forward is your wife...and the mother of your child." She held her breath as an array of expressions ran over his face.

Alan's heart thumped. Elation filled him. His eyes clouded with tears of joy. He pressed his mouth to hers as they tumbled together to the sandy beach.

The future promised a lifetime of love, laughter, challenges and adventure, no matter which roles they chose.

The follow-up to *Sweet Surrender*
and *Here and Now...*

*Straight* to the
**Heart**

Bestselling author

# MICHELLE MONKOU

Fearful that her unsavory past is about to be exposed,
hip-hop diva Stacy Watts dates clean-cut Omar Masterson
to save her new image. But their playacting backfires
when their mutual attraction starts to burn out of control!
Now Stacy must fight to keep the secrets of her past
from destroying her future with Omar.

*Available the first week of September
wherever books are sold.*

KIMANI™
ROMANCE

**www.kimanipress.com**

KPMM0340907

He was the first man to touch her soul...

SOUL
Caress

Favorite author

KIM SHAW

When privileged Kennedy Daniels loses her sight,
hospital orderly Malik Crawford helps heal her
wounds and awaken her desire. But they come from
different worlds, so unless Kennedy's willing to defy her
prominent family, a future between them is impossible.

*Available the first week of September
wherever books are sold.*

KIMANI™
ROMANCE

National bestselling author

# KIM LOUISE

## *Ever Wonderful*

When his truck hits Ariana Macleod's prized Angus, Braxton Ambrose goes to work on her ranch to repay her. Handsome Brax's presence feels very welcome to Ariana—especially when their mutual attraction explodes into a sizzling affair. Brax isn't the settling-down type, but when tragedy strikes, he's determined to convince Ariana that he'll be with her for the long haul.

"Heartbreaking, heartwarming and downright funny, this story will totally captivate any reader from beginning to end."
—*Romantic Times BOOKreviews* on *True Devotion*

**Available the first week of September, wherever books are sold.**

**ARABESQUE®**

**www.kimanipress.com**　　KPKL0180907